Aug 14

THE TERROR OF THE TENGU

BY JOHN SEVEN

STONE ARCH BOOKS
a capstone imprint

The Time-Tripping Faradays
are published by Stone Arch Books
A Capstone Imprint
1710 Roe Crest Drive
North Mankato, Minnesota 56003
www.capstonepub.com

Library of Congress Cataloging-in-Publication Data

Seven, John, author.
The terror of the tengu / by John Seven; illustrated by Stephanie Hans.
    pages cm. -- (The time-tripping Faradays; 3)
  Summary: When twenty-fifth century time travelers Dawkins and
Hypatia find a plastic artifact among the Neanderthals, it is an anomaly--
but on their next assignment to Japan in 1595 they find much more
significant evidence of tampering, using virtual reality to induce belief in
a demon tengu, and causing mass hysteria.
  ISBN 978-1-4342-9173-8 (library binding) -- ISBN 978-1-62370-110-9
(paper over board) -- ISBN 978-1-4342-9175-2 (pbk.) -- ISBN 978-1-4965-
0101-1 (ebook)
1. Time travel--Juvenile fiction. 2. Virtual reality--Juvenile fiction. 3.
Tengu--Juvenile fiction. 4. Adventure stories. 5. Japan--History--Azuchi-
Momoyama period, 1568-1603--Juvenile fiction. [1. Time travel--Fiction. 2.
Virtual reality--Fiction. 3. Tengu--Fiction. 4. Adventure and adventurers--
Fiction. 5. Science fiction. 6. Japan--History--16th century--Fiction.] I.
Hans, Stephanie, illustrator. II. Title.
  PZ7.S5145Te 2014
  813.6--dc23

                    2013047089

Cover illustration: Stephanie Hans

Designer: Kay Fraser

Photo-Vector Credits: Shutterstock

Printed in China by Nordica
0414/CA21400609
032014   008095NORDF14

FOR HARRY AND HUGO

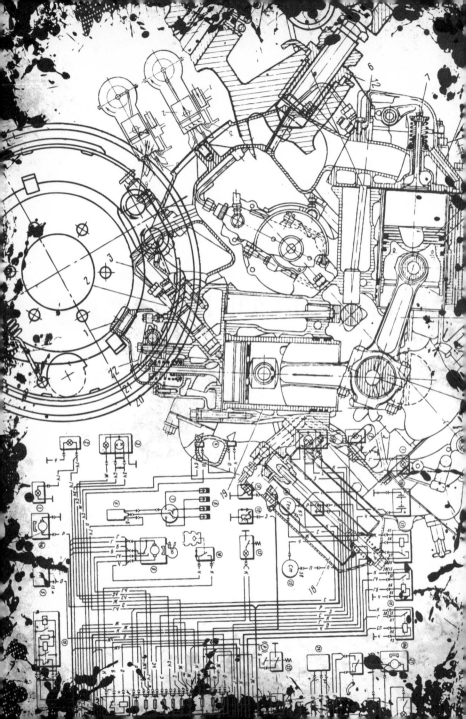

CHAPTER

1

From under a tree, Dawk stared blankly over at the group of Neanderthals. They were huddled together next to a crude shelter fashioned from the skeleton of a mammoth, leaves and skins draped on top, right next to some caves in a wooded ridge.

Neanderthals weren't so bad. They weren't very exciting either. But they weren't so bad.

His mom and dad probably didn't agree. All they cared about was footwear—shoes, boots, sandals, slippers, and whatever else their employers, the Cosmos Institute in the twenty-fifth century, wanted to know more about. Whenever the Cosmos Institute needed to learn about footwear, they sent the Faraday family back in time to study. With this mission, the idea was to try to decide once and for all if twelve thousand years ago, European Neanderthals had any sort of foot coverings and, if so, when they started wearing those foot coverings.

So far, the Neanderthals were completely barefoot, and Mom and Dad were annoyed.

"They don't even tie leaves to their feet!" Mom complained. "Not even leaves!"

"I saw one fellow rub his feet, a woman pull pebbles from between her toes, and a child extract a thorn or two, but none of them thought maybe they should cover their feet," Dad added. "And I can't force them to! This is hopeless. I'm tired of living on berries and whatever burned meat we can coax away from the Neanderthals."

"Trying to pinpoint the moment Neanderthals adopted footwear, if they ever did, is about as difficult as singling out one specific nanocircuit in the whole DataVerse," Mom said, sighing.

Dawk's sister, Hype, was sitting in on what

appeared to be a Neanderthal craft circle down near the water. Their computer-generated escort, Fizzbin, had warned her not to get too creative—if she did, it might throw a time anomaly into the visit. Hype just followed the Neanderthals' lead, making a kind of crude jewelry that never once appeared to be made by someone cleverer than anyone else there.

Dawk shot a message to some of his Link friends.

You should see this mammoth-skeleton house—way better than any of our quarters in the Alvarium. It has to be in a PlayMod. (Dawk)

Bring back a real mammoth skeleton and we'll make one of those in the center of the Mall. (Link friend)

I can't bring back bones! And those are big bones! (Dawk)

We can use them as Bone Man bait! (Link friend)

One moment later, there was an invite into the latest reno of the *Bone Man: Alvarium of Terror* PlayMod, another variation of the bone-eating-human urban legend that all the kids in the twenty-fifth century loved to scare each other with. Dawk was just about to enter the game when he heard screaming coming from the Neanderthal settlement.

I'll face Bone Man later. (Dawk)

It was Hype, struggling with a Neanderthal woman over some small item. Crafting circle disputes could get pretty nasty, so Dawk rushed over.

"I said you can't use that!" Hype yelled, trying to pull something away from the woman. "That doesn't belong in a necklace!"

The OpBot, a tiny flying robot that was Fizzbin's eyes and ears on the family's time travels, started buzzing around Hype's hands.

If you can hold it still for a moment, I can cross-reference the item in the history banks. (Fizzbin)

She's in a fight, Fizzbin. I doubt she can hold it still for a moment. (Dawk)

Excuse me. I don't have arms, so I'm not always clear on how they work. (Fizzbin)

Dawk firmly took hold of both Hype's arm and the Neanderthal woman's. It turned out they were having a tug-of-war over a small white object. It had a slight gleam in the sunlight and looked man-made.

The OpBot glided over long enough for a quick scan, and Fizzbin made a match almost immediately.

Spork. (Fizzbin)

What? (Hype)

Is that the Neanderthal woman's name? (Dawk)

No. You are fighting over a spork. A plastic spork. It is an eating utensil common in the late twentieth and early twenty-first centuries, but dating back to the late nineteenth century in its pre-plastic form. It was particularly convenient for travel food of different varieties, providing humans with one variety of cutlery where, at a proper meal, there would be two. You could eat soup and salad with the same utensil. Very ingenious. (Fizzbin)

Maybe there is something we can trade her for the spork? If it's from the twentieth century, it's causing a temporal anomaly and disrupting history. (Hype)

Perhaps. However, I can't find anything in the history banks about a stray spork discovered at any point and turning archaeological theory on its head. (Fizzbin)

We could try to trade for it, but all we've got to work with is the OpBot. I have a feeling that when it comes to causing a temporal anomaly and disrupting history, a tiny floating robot with a temporal data link to the twenty-fifth century is a lot worse than a spork, right? (Dawk)

Dawk was right, so the only real option was to grab Hype's hands and help her pull harder. The spork was slipping out of the Neanderthal woman's grasp when Mom and Dad came running over.

You really shouldn't fight with the Neanderthals, Hype. (Dad)

I'm trying to save history! (Hype)

Mom and Dad joined in. All four Faradays tried their best to pull the tiny spork from the Neanderthal woman's grasp. When it finally came loose with a sudden jolt, each family member plummeted backward into the dirt.

What is that thing? A tiny shovel? (Mom)

No. A spork. Probably from the twentieth century. Doesn't belong in this era at all. That's why I was trying to get it. (Hype)

What is a Neanderthal doing with a spork? (Dad)

Not eating soup and salad, that's for sure. (Dawk)

The family climbed off of the ground while the Neanderthal woman made a big fuss, snarling out something that sounded like an angry song. Neanderthals had a language, but not much was known about it, so it wasn't translatable to the Faradays.

The pre-programmed NeuroTranslators that were patched through the frontal lobe of the brain allowed time travelers like the Faradays to speak whatever language they needed to speak flawlessly without having to learn it. But the NeuroTranslators didn't work with Neanderthal grunts and wheezes. Still, even without the translators, Dawk was pretty sure that she was probably screaming something like, "That's my spork! Give me back my spork!"

I am alerting Benton. He'll have you out of there momentarily. (Fizzbin)

Because of this? (Dad)

A bit of Neanderthal trouble usually wouldn't be enough of a reason to have you transported out, but given the appearance of the spork more than ten thousand years before it should exist, yes. (Fizzbin)

We haven't witnessed even the slightest desire on the part of the Neanderthals to put anything on their feet. Will the Chancellor be upset? (Dad)

You haven't done anything wrong. If anything, this will bring you one step closer to getting out of the footwear studies department. Expect the temporal passage shortly. (Fizzbin)

A large male Neanderthal peeked out of the mammoth-skeleton house. He looked concerned. He crept slowly toward the family, his eyes darting between the spork in Hype's hand and the other Faradays.

Dawk figured he was sizing them up and trying to decide if he could win in a fight. But as the temporal passage materialized around the family, the Neanderthal man looked confused. That made sense. The passage collapsed the dimension of time in the area, making the space there appear wrinkled.

It turned out that the Neanderthal man was braver and more determined than the Faradays or Fizzbin expected. As the current era faded away around them, the Neanderthal bolted for Hype—or, specifically, for the spork, grabbing it and trying to pull it out of her hands.

When he touched her, the temporal passage

expanded around him. Hype tried to pull the spork away from him, but he wouldn't let go.

And then everything was gone. It was the Faradays and the spork and the Neanderthal floating together in a moment of all time happening at once as the tech guys in the twenty-fifth century steered them toward the right nanoparticles. As the automated buildup of the dimension of time began, they began to be pulled into the proper doorway to go home.

The Neanderthal looked like he was panicking, though, and let go of the spork. Hype reached out, trying to grab onto him, but she missed. He faded away into the blank glob of time even as the Faradays took form back in the Alvarium in the twenty-fifth century.

Hype, stunned and with wet eyes, held up the spork. "I think I lost the Neanderthal. But I saved this."

CHAPTER

2

Dawk rushed around the corridors of the Alvarium as fast as he could, eyes peeled for Hype.

Where was she hiding?

Benton, who oversaw all the temporal missions, expected the family for a briefing on their next one, to Japan, but no one could find Hype, not even on the Link.

I suppose she must have set her access to private. (Mom)

She's upset about what happened to the Neanderthal. (Dad)

But Benton said he wasn't dead, right? Just . . . what did he say? (Dawk)

Living an eternal moment until he slips back somewhere in the actual fabric of time. (Fizzbin)

Benton had told them that the Neanderthal was floating like a temporal ghost between the nanoparticles that created the flow of time. Benton promised to do everything he could to pull the Neanderthal out of it, but he couldn't guarantee anything, since the Neanderthal didn't have a neural bypass that could be easily tracked.

"Whenever a section of time manifests itself solidly, it's possible he will collide with that and be dumped out of the vortex," Benton said. "Or some other manifestation if that one doesn't happen. Foreign bodies are generally expelled sooner or later. For that poor guy's sake, I hope it's sooner."

So Hype felt bad.

She felt like it was her fault, and she wanted some time alone.

But Dawk knew she needed to talk it out, so he was barreling through the Alvarium, looking for her with the OpBot alongside him.

The passages and open spaces of the Alvarium usually didn't have many people in them and were often just empty. There wasn't much for people to do or look at.

Dawk knew the Alvarium like the back of his hand but still couldn't say much about how it looked, even after fourteen years of living in it in between temporal assignments. It looked gray. And maybe tan. Not too inspiring. No wonder everyone was tuned out and concentrating on vReality mods and other things on the Link.

Dawk stepped out onto an aerial bridge that crossed the top section of the Alvarium and looked down into the huge open public center called the Mall.

There were some people out, reclining on the couches that were all over the place. These days, the Mall was mostly used as a change of scenery for anyone tired of spending their time on the Link in the privacy of their rooms. The current visitors all looked like they were asleep.

Then Dawk spied Hype.

"Hey, Hype!" he screamed. "Hype!"

Dawk's voice echoed through the Mall. Hype looked up.

"Stay there, Hype!" Dawk yelled down. "Do not move!"

He worked his way down to the Mall as fast as he could.

"If you'd just not keep your Link status to private, I wouldn't have to yell to you like I was some kind of crazy person," Dawk said when he got to his sister.

"I was just visiting Ezrine," Hype said, motioning to a girl on the couch next to her. "Or trying to. Thought I'd say hi to her face."

Ezrine had been Hype's best friend forever, but the more time Hype spent traveling through time with her family, the more time Ezrine spent in PlayMods, having fun in vRealities and meeting other people on the Link. They had barely spoken while Hype was with the Neanderthals.

"Her face doesn't seem to notice you," Dawk said.

Hype sighed. "I haven't gotten more than two words out of her, and those were 'hold on,' which she said about fifteen minutes ago. Haven't seen her in ages, and now I'm sitting next to her, trying to talk to her on-Link. That's why I'm set for private. I scanned the PlayMod roles to see why she was so hard to reach, and get this—she's playing five of them."

"Five PlayMods at once?"

"Multi-PlayModding. Everyone seems to be doing it. You think Ezrine is the only friend I've tried to meet up with? Three others before her, all multi-PlayModding. Horrible for conversation."

Hype sighed again, while Ezrine began waving her arms and moving on the couch. That's what people looked like when they were on NeuroNet overload. It used to be a rare thing, but was getting more common all the time.

"Have you ever really looked around the Alvarium?" Hype said. "I've noticed some things while I've been sitting here. Like windows."

"What windows?" Dawk said.

"Exactly. Do you ever wonder why we don't have any windows in the Alvarium?"

"Because no one makes curtains anymore,"

Dawk answered, "so there's no use for windows. A thing of the past."

That's not exactly accurate. The lack of windows is actually because of the gamma ray burst and the resulting destruction of the ozone, combined with the earlier warming of— (Fizzbin)

Not the time for environmental science, Fizzbin. (Dawk)

"And what about below the Mall?" Hype asked. "Seems like there should be something below the Mall, right? Every time we visit somewhere, it seems like there's something below where we are, something hidden, some maze."

"Listen, Benton wants us," Dawk said. "Right now. You weren't on-Link, so . . . here I am."

Hype's face lit up. "Has Benton said anything about tracking down the source of the spork? Is it related to other items we've found from the future?"

In past missions, Dawk and Hype had found evidence of time travelers from the future interfering with history. They had even met one of the mysterious future travelers when they went to ancient Rome.

"When you compare it to time-jumping gadgets and robots in dragon form, a spork doesn't seem very important," Dawk said. "Come on, Benton's waiting."

"Maybe I should've just let the Neanderthal woman have the spork," Hype said glumly. She stood up. "So what if it ended up on jewelry? Would that really have changed history?"

"Maybe the history of jewelry," Dawk said. "And who cares about that?"

CHAPTER

3

When Dawk and Hype arrived at Benton's, Mom and Dad were already sitting down and practicing manners for their upcoming mission to medieval Japan.

"Japan is never an easy trip," Benton told the Faradays sternly. "You'll need to save an enormous amount of customs and etiquette to your NeuroCaches for instant access, but we'll also have to practice more common ones before you go. You need to have an idea of what will be expected from you in order to maintain the roles you will play."

Benton pulled a cup of coffee from his NutroFabricator and took a sip.

"Also," he continued, "we felt that, in this particular case, it was best to say you are from a country that does not really exist, so there would be no double-checking with any real monarchs. Japan is far enough from Europe that with the right documents, medieval citizens will accept Alvarium as a real European country. The country of Alvarium has been placed in a few texts in history, just to give it some weight. Nothing major, no time discrepancies, but there is now a trail in the history books."

"That's pretty cool," Dawk said.

"Now," said Benton, "shall we practice? The information is now accessible in your NeuroCaches, and you will need it to act out some scenarios for me. Several times."

Dawk and Hype looked at each other. They had never had to practice manners and customs before a mission.

"Wouldn't it just be easier to stick us in a vReality module for this?" asked Dawk.

"Perhaps," Benton said, "but it wouldn't be as much fun for me. Now, shall we?"

CHAPTER

4

The Faradays had to walk to Lord Sanada's castle from a distance. Benton usually aimed time-traveling arrivals close to their mission site. And usually, that meant they'd land in a bathroom or a closet. But, he explained, that wouldn't work in medieval Japan. The Faraday family had to be seen walking to the castle.

"The castle was so well guarded and the inside of the castle so confusing that it would be very suspicious if there was no record of your arrival through all the checkpoints," Benton had told them.

"And that includes the checkpoints called the eyes of the citizenry."

So the family had to walk to their mission from a distance. And normally, they wouldn't mind, but normally, they weren't wearing little wooden sandals that were unbearably uncomfortable.

Usually, the Visual Cortex Shells did the work of making time travelers appear to be dressed in appropriate clothing, including shoes. But as was custom in medieval Japan, the Faradays would be required to take off and put on their shoes almost constantly.

Though the Shells could be programmed to switch from shoes to the traditional socks known as *tabi*, Benton had decided that it would look weird if the family's shoes just disappeared. The action of taking off one's shoes was just as important as not wearing them. And so the four Faradays would just have to deal with changing their own footwear on this trip.

It was just one more thing for Dawk to complain about as they walked through the fairy tale-like forest toward Numata Castle.

It turned out that medieval Japan was very pretty. All kinds of small, colorful houses, with white paper placed over their window and door areas instead of glass, were lining the way. There were more houses, and they became closer together, as the family drew nearer to the castle. And soon, there were more people. Most of the people stared at the Faradays silently with curious gazes.

All four of the Faradays were quiet too, enjoying the moment that only came once for each mission, when the past was new and strange and a little bit scary.

Everyone knew pretty much everyone else in the Alvarium, and there were no surprises. It was fun to be strangers in a new place.

I would suggest not speaking to anyone. The castle towns of this era had designated areas for various social ranks, and the closer we get, the higher the rank. I could have had customs for each level sent to your neural bypasses, so that you behave properly, but my feeling is that direct communication will just delay our mission. (Fizzbin)

Soon, Numata Castle lay ahead of them, but it was not at all like any castle they had seen before. It had a bright red pagoda tower that looked like a bunch of elegant houses piled up on top of one another, each with lovely triangular roofs shielding little patios that came out from its center.

This looks so much nicer than European castles, don't you think? It has more character, and it's so much cleaner. The Holy Roman Empire's castles just can't compare. (Mom)

I'm sure the dank quality of Prague doesn't speak for the entire empire. But it would take an effort for them to match this. (Dad)

My feet hurt. (Dawk)

There was a moat at the base of the castle and a guard's gate just before it. When the Faradays reached the gate, a soldier inside popped his head out.

"Welcome to the first gate. Please state your business," he said.

"We are the ministers of foot coverings from the faraway land of Alvarium." Dad smiled. "Lord Sanada expects us."

"Pass and stop at the second gate, please," the guard told them.

The family moved down the path and found there were many more gates beyond the second one. Between the gates were winding pathways and halls, plus little garden areas with resting places, as if visitors regularly became so exhausted while entering the castle that they needed a break now and then.

How much farther is it? Can I sit on one of those benches? (Dawk)

Let me guess. Your feet hurt. (Hype)

Yes. They do. (Dawk)

I am truly sorry that there is no CartoMod available for this locale. You're going to pass through a further series of courtyards and passages before you reach another wall, which will lead to the center courtyard. (Fizzbin)

Then are we there? (Dawk)

The central courtyard is where you will find Lord Sanada's quarters, including his receiving room, where the tea ceremony will take place upon introduction. (Fizzbin)

Are all castles in Japan this difficult to get into? (Dawk)

The good ones are. (Fizzbin)

CHAPTER 5

Once they made it to the central courtyard, Dawk and Hype could see that the pagoda tower was even more impressive close up. There were other, smaller bungalows surrounding it.

An attendant led the Faraday family toward a fragile, modest-looking wooden structure that had white paper covering its windows. It was preceded by a small area of carefully arranged rocks that the attendant tiptoed through before stopping at a small basin next to the little house.

Following the introduction to Lord Sanada, there will

be a tea ceremony. I advise you to say little and follow Sanada's lead. It is a delicate and important ritual for samurai and Japanese society in general, so best not to disrupt it and jeopardize the whole mission. (Fizzbin)

"Please," the attendant said, and nodded toward the basin.

He's blocking the entrance. We can't go in. (Hype)

That's because you are expected to wash your hands and mouths here before you enter. (Fizzbin)

The Faradays washed, nervous that they'd make a mistake. When they were all done, the man beckoned them through the sliding door and inside, where five mats were placed on the floor around a very short table.

Nod your heads politely and go to your mats. Say nothing. Do not sit. Let your faces reflect patience and tranquility. (Fizzbin)

How long are we staying here? Do we have to do this every day? Where are the samurai fights? (Dawk)

Time to change into tabi, *Faradays. Get those shoes off your feet now and replace them with the ceremonial socks. (Fizzbin)*

Every member of the family fumbled with the

shoes. Though they looked perfectly easy to take off, the Faradays just weren't used to the wooden shoes. Hype felt sure they all looked like idiots as they tried to slip on their socks delicately.

We practiced the sitting. Please get it right, Faradays. (Fizzbin)

Hype had to admit that this whole experience was already grueling. It would have taken a lot of discipline to live in this world. She couldn't wait until they were brought to their quarters and could just do whatever they wanted without having to first go through the extensive etiquette database that sat in her NeuroCache.

She sat down on her knees, as was required of tea ceremony guests.

Suddenly, a sharp pole with a curve at one end was thrust through the thin wall of the bungalow.

Are we under attack? (Hype)

I hope not. We just got here. (Mom)

Whoever had stuck the pole in was trying to pull it out, but the curved end made it difficult.

The little house began to rattle.

Hype was beginning to suspect that there

wouldn't be a tea ceremony. Once someone decked out in gray samurai armor fell through the wall and landed on the teahouse floor, she felt pretty convinced.

Hype looked down at the fallen warrior and then looked up as another samurai in red and black armor barreled through the newly made hole in the wall.

This is the best tea ceremony I've ever been to! (Dawk)

Please, everyone, stay out of the way of that sword pole thing. The way he's swinging it around, someone could lose an eye or an ear or a head! (Mom)

Remember, according to the etiquette of the court, it is probably not in your best interest to flee for safety. Stay calm. One desperate move could undo all of Benton's planning. (Fizzbin)

The gray samurai on the floor moved his pole weapon left and right in a choppy way, attempting to knock the red and black warrior down to the knees.

But the red and black warrior jumped out of the pole's way to avoid contact.

Well, almost. One chop finally connected, and

the red and black samurai came crashing into a shelf on the far side of the room. All the material for the tea ceremony came down, shattering and scattering across the room.

This gave the gray samurai a chance to get up quickly and move over to the red and black one, slumped against the shelf.

But suddenly, the red and black samurai, without even looking, whipped the pole back between the legs of the gray samurai, who tripped and went flying into the other wall. The gray samurai put a crack in that wall and then slowly slid down onto the floor.

The red and black samurai took a deep breath before climbing off of the shattered tea set.

"I will have to have those walls repaired before Lord Sanada returns from his mission," said the samurai, pulling off the helmet to reveal the face of a calm woman.

"I am Komatsuhime, lady of Numata Castle," she said, smiling. "Forgive me, I was not informed of this meeting until my daily maneuvers had begun. My sparring partner, Shinobu, takes his role very seriously, and it would have been impolite to put a stop to our battle."

Komatsuhime closed her eyes and bowed her head. "Now, once this mess is tidied and Shinobu removed, I believe I owe you a tea ceremony."

CHAPTER

6

For the week following their arrival, the Faradays' stay was as tranquil as the grounds of the castle. But Hype knew there was some energy lurking under the calm, thanks to Komatsuhime's entrance at the tea ceremony, and she wanted to get closer to that energy.

Hype's parents had gotten to work pretty quickly. Komatsuhime had handed them over to one of her assistants in the castle and given them the run of the place—shoe-wise, at least. Mom and Dad had actually told Hype that having to wear the real footwear of the era on their feet had given them a whole new appreciation for the work they were doing.

Dawk spent most of his time exploring the castle town, but Hype was too intrigued by Komatsuhime to leave the castle. Hype spent her days wandering around the castle, hoping to bump into the imposing woman. The way that Komatsuhime had just come barreling in there, waving that odd staff at her sparring partner, had been beyond amazing.

One afternoon, Hype saw Komatsuhime standing next to a little stone structure with a small flame on the top end, staring down at it like she was deep in thought. She was dressed in elegant, colorful robes, quite different from the rough armor Hype had first seen her wearing. Hype rushed over, hoping Komatsuhime wouldn't be annoyed. After the samurai battle she'd seen, there was no way she wanted to risk annoying Komatsuhime.

I need a conversation starter, Fizzbin. (Hype)

Gardens have a very important role in this culture. You could just comment on how natural the garden looks. That's always a good starting place. (Fizzbin)

The woman turned and looked at Hype, then smiled, nodded her head, and turned back to the stone structure.

"Your garden looks very natural," Hype said.

"It is not my garden, really," Komatsuhime said, "but I do oversee its upkeep, and so I appreciate your compliment."

"Is that what you were doing, checking to make sure it has been taken care of properly?"

Komatsuhime gestured to the stone structure. "No, no, this lantern started my mind off in a certain direction. I was allowing it to continue going that way."

"It's a very beautiful lantern," Hype said. "It certainly inspires my mind . . . to . . . think."

Would you like help? (Fizzbin)

No, I can do this. (Hype)

"And what does the lantern inspire your mind to think about?" Komatsuhime asked.

"That I know a lot of people who have never seen an actual flame," Hype answered.

Komatsuhime looked at her curiously. "Are you from a very wet place?" she asked.

"No, Alvarium isn't wet, just strange," Hype said. "What does the lantern make you think of?"

"It makes me think that each of us have aspects of the four elements within us. Earth, water, fire, wind; it is all there at once, but sometimes any one of them is hidden by the others. Every person hides one of their elements."

"My guess is that the one you hide must be fire," Hype said.

Komatsuhime smiled. "And how did you guess that?"

"Because I saw it burst out of you when you sparred in the teahouse. You were filled with fire."

"I should not burden you with my secrets," Komatsuhime said as her sparring partner, Shinobu, entered the garden.

"Pardon, Lady Komatsuhime," he said. "I need to speak with you about incidents in the castle town. More property has been destroyed in the night."

Komatsuhime nodded politely and then turned to Hype. "Forgive me. I have work I must attend to." She turned to walk away with Shinobu, but stopped when Hype spoke again.

"Can we talk again tomorrow?" Hype asked. "I'm sorry, that's not rude, is it?"

"I will come to the lantern again tomorrow at the same time," Komatsuhime said and then walked away.

CHAPTER

7

The next day, Hype was waiting, and this time she was prepared with questions. She had spent some time on NeuroPedia trying to figure out just how a woman became a samurai.

It turned out that women samurai were known as the *onna-bugeisha*, the warrior women of medieval Japan. Komatsuhime had probably trained all her life to become one. Tearing down teahouses, Hype decided, must be a way of keeping her skills up to date.

There was a lot Hype wanted to know about

Komatsuhime's life, and she hoped it wasn't rude to ask about it directly.

She gazed at the garden as she waited. Soon, Komatsuhime came out of a doorway on the far end of the courtyard and acknowledged Hype with a slight nod.

"I hope I'm not bothering you," Hype said.

"The company of a friendly person is a delight after sitting all day managing the affairs of the castle," Komatsuhime said. "So many things to organize. Like repairs. I have an entire teahouse wall that needs workmen to attend to it, you know." She smiled.

Hype laughed and thought, *She's getting comfortable with me.*

"Are you bored with your duties as the lady of the castle?" Hype asked.

"No," Komatsuhime said. "Well, yes. Rather, I am not ashamed of them, nor do I hold them any grudge, but they take up so much time. There is more to me than schedules and billing—oh, and guiding Shinobu on how to handle thefts of food and such crime in the town. Some there claim a monster, some *yokai* or another, is on the loose. And of course they want the lord of the castle to do something about that."

A quick NeuroPedia search showed Hype that yokai were demons, and there were hundreds of different kinds. Demons were make-believe monsters that did bad things to humans, a common belief in various human cultures long before the twenty-fifth century.

"What could the lord of the castle do, exactly?" Hype asked.

"Hunt it down and display the carcass as proof the townspeople are safe," Komatsuhime said. "If it is actually a monster and not a spirit, that is. But the lord is away, and the lady has too many mundane things to do, even if she were up for a monster hunt."

"All of your duties don't give you the chance to pursue your other interests? Like fighting and monster hunting?"

"My husband is very understanding and very forgiving of my need to continue my training, and for that, I am grateful. But I've had my fair share of action, and sometimes I do miss that. Sometimes, I can do what I want, but most of the time I must remain a dutiful and well-behaved wife. And so I am."

"A dutiful wife who's pretty handy with a . . . a . . ."

The weapon name you are searching for is naginata. *(Fizzbin)*

". . . a naginata. How did you get to be such an expert at handling it?"

Komatsuhime chuckled. "I have been trained since I was a small girl, with a naginata suited for one so tiny. Perhaps you are interested yourself in learning how to brandish a naginata? The onna-bugeisha warriors have many skills that you might enjoy."

Hype was thrilled. Was Komatsuhime offering her onna-bugeisha training?

"I'm not very interested in teaching a young woman the art of flower arrangement," the older woman continued, "but I would like to train someone."

It sounds like she wants . . . girl time? (Hype)

"I would love that, Komatsuhime-san," Hype said.

"Then we will start tomorrow morning, Hypatia-san."

This was great. Beyond great. It meant so many great things, one of which was that Hype was pretty sure the samurai skills she'd learn would make Dawk speechless.

For once.

CHAPTER

8

Is Hype still lurking around trying to get the attention of that lady samurai? (Dawk)

It appears she has made friendly contact with the young woman. Hype just asked me for a weapon's name. (Fizzbin)

Hype's asking about weapons? That's completely not like her. (Dawk)

Dawk was wandering out of the castle. He'd finally mastered the exit path with Fizzbin's help after a day of trying to find his way out. Dawk decided he would take it upon himself to explore the castle town and help map it out for his family. It would at least help the time pass.

Japan is making me a nervous wreck. I never know when I'm supposed to bow or take off my shoes or not say something. Or say something. This is like another world. (Dawk)

Close enough. It's not as rigid or difficult as Benton would have you believe. Maybe you need to ease into the culture. Perhaps an afternoon at the Noh theater. I can lead you to the entertainment district. A fun and restful way to take in the current culture of Japan. (Fizzbin)

I don't know if I'm in the mood for that. What's it like? (Dawk)

Theater is like a PlayMod that you can't take part in. It happens a few feet in front of your eyes instead of through your neural bypass. (Fizzbin)

Dawk figured he might as well do something. The walk would take him to the other side of the castle perimeter to a neighborhood that was new to him, so he would get to see another view of life in 1595 Japan.

The merchant district that Dawk walked through was far busier than the area where the family had first arrived. That area had been where the upper-level samurai lived. This was way more interesting. Dawk noticed a bookstore and, next to it, children crowded around a little kiosk that had puppets acting out a story.

That's like a sixteenth-century PlayMod! (Dawk)

Perhaps you'd like to go to the bookstore and make a reading purchase? I could easily have Japanese written language recognition put on your NeuroCache for you to access as needed. (Fizzbin)

One ancient entertainment technology at a time, Fizzbin. (Dawk)

Dawk wandered over to the Noh theater, which was really a small outdoor stage covered by an ornate roof, with seating around it. It looked like an open version of Sanada's teahouse. Dawk sat down on a bench.

This feels weird. I just sit here? (Dawk)

As the play progresses, you will settle into it. (Fizzbin)

People really like just sitting back and watching? They don't want to get in there and be part of it? (Dawk)

I suppose that happens sometimes, but usually, no. (Fizzbin)

So how do you affect the characters by sitting out here? (Dawk)

You don't. (Fizzbin)

You mean the characters just do whatever they want and you don't have any way to change it? (Dawk)

It's a limited means of storytelling, that is certainly true. (Fizzbin)

Makes you appreciate PlayMods even more. (Dawk)

There were a few other people who filed in, including a scruffy man in armor and dirty robes who sat next to Dawk. The man brought with him a noticeable stink.

Would it be rude to scoot over a few seats to escape the smell? (Dawk)

The man is wearing armor. Perhaps best not to offend him. (Fizzbin)

The man pulled off his little round cap and scratched his scraggily head. "Most people are too scared to come out of their homes to attend the theater," he said. "I won't let some yokai keep me away from my favorite show."

"Me neither," Dawk said. "Yokai don't intimidate me."

What are yokai? (Dawk)

Yokai are a form of demons or supernatural monsters in Japanese mythology. (Fizzbin)

When did humans stop believing in fake, silly legends, anyhow? (Dawk)

We'll know someday after the Bone Man you love to talk about is never mentioned on the Link again. (Fizzbin)

"You have any snacks?" the man said, turning to Dawk.

"Snacks?" asked Dawk.

"Snacks. Food. Food for the theater."

"Sorry, no snacks here," Dawk told him. "Maybe someone else has some."

"I just like a little something at the theater. It helps you enjoy the full experience, and it also means I have a little something in my belly for the journey back. No fun collapsing on rural roads."

What happens if I change seats? Will that insult him? (Dawk)

I don't find any rules against it, but then again, some manners are regional, so I can't say for sure. (Fizzbin)

So I'm stuck sitting here just in case? (Dawk)

It appears so. (Fizzbin)

"Have you seen this before?" the man asked. "'The Long-Nosed Goblin in Kurama.' This is the one *noh* that always calls to me whenever I am in town. Any other, I can resist, but this one? Never. Do you know why?"

"No."

"Because I have to face those goblins, those *tengu*, every day of my life on the mountain. The tengu even follow me into town. Big, bad tengu. I like to duck into a noh so I can lose it in the crowd. It won't notice me in here. But I'll see that big-nosed goblin."

Dawk stared at the man.

"I am Nazo. I am a *yamabushi*, you see, follower of Shugendo, seeker of enlightenment," he said, bowing his head. "And enemy to those bulb-nosed tengu."

Oh, this is very interesting. A yamabushi is a warrior monk from the mountains who travels around on spiritual missions and, most fascinatingly, fights demons. How exciting! It's such a shame demons don't really exist. (Fizzbin)

Tell me more. (Dawk)

Yamabushi are fierce fighters and have magical powers. Well, if magic existed, they would. His mortal enemy is a tengu, a demon with many forms whose only purpose is to bother yamabushi. (Fizzbin)

If demons existed, that is. (Dawk)

Exactly. (Fizzbin)

"Hey!" the man said. "After the performance, you take me out and buy a snack. Deal? I can pay you back by healing something you have wrong with you or making contact with a dead friend if you want. Maybe I can conjure something! Whatever sounds good to you."

There was a loud groan from the monk's stomach.

"You couldn't just conjure a snack?" Dawk asked.

The monk patted his stomach, laughed, and then punched Dawk on the shoulder.

"Being hungry can make you a little funny." He pointed to his head. "But I'm okay in there. Don't worry."

CHAPTER 9

After the play, Dawk followed Nazo out of the theater with the rest of the crowd. The monk looked side to side, suspiciously. "Maybe I lost him," he muttered.

"In the play, the tengu is pretty nice," Dawk said. "I thought you said they were nasty monsters."

"That play is for children," Nazo said. "Doesn't want to scare them, so it makes the tengu seem tricky instead of evil. How about tricky and evil? Oh, what I wouldn't give for an *umeboshi*."

"Is that a weapon?"

The monk stared at him.

That's a pickled plum. The taste bud analyses we conducted on you lead me to believe that you not would care for them. (Fizzbin)

"Oh, an UM-eboshi," said Dawk with a laugh. "Sorry, I got that mixed up with a . . . with . . . another thing that sounds very similar, but is very different."

"You're an odd one," the monk said. "Funny, a yamabushi calling someone odd. I know we yamabushi are odd, but that's the price of being mystical and spiritually aware, walking a magical path, and knowing all the creatures we know, good and evil. Plus refusing worldly pleasures. But you—you are very strange on a whole other level."

"So, you say that a tengu has been following you down from the mountain?" asked Dawk. "Sounds dangerous."

"Ripping the town apart while it looks for me. It went through a shoe-repair shop last night. Tengu are beyond dangerous, but that does not stop me from using all my training and powers to fend him off."

"Why is he chasing you?"

"Why isn't he, that's the question! This particular type of tengu hate my kind and take their revenge by appearing to be one of us. Of course, I can tell the difference, as can so many others of my order. There are differences!"

"Like what?"

"Height!" Nazo shouted. "Tengu are notoriously tall. And wings! But these are often hidden beneath cloaks. That's not important, though, because their huge noses are the real giveaway. Huge noses, like nothing you've ever seen! Noses so large they could be weapons!"

Are there any PlayMods with tengu? I'd like to see one. (Dawk)

None currently. Perhaps you could help develop one with the information you are gathering. (Fizzbin)

"So you said you live on a mountain?" Dawk asked.

"Mount Takao. Less than a day's hike from here. Crawling with tengu. You can't swing a naginata there without hitting one. Of course, you want to hit them with naginata."

The deeper levels of the bio-history banks reveal that Mount Takao in Japan was at one time home to unusually enormous flying squirrels called musasabi. *Probably his tengu. (Fizzbin)*

What is a flying squirrel? (Dawk)

Fizzbin shot a picture to Dawk's NeuroCache.

Looks like a rat with extra arm skin and a big bushy tail. No wonder he's afraid of them. (Dawk)

Nazo stopped with a sudden jerk.

"What—" Dawk started to speak, but Nazo covered Dawk's mouth with one hand and then pointed in the short distance with the other.

Dawk could just make out a figure in the shadow of a tent. He couldn't see much, but the size of the nose was pretty obvious.

"Found him," Nazo said. The monk gripped his naginata. "Follow me, slowly," he said.

Nazo crept ahead, and Dawk followed.

"How do you defeat a tengu?" Dawk asked.

"You scare it. You poke it on the nose. You steal its magic gourd. Maybe vanquish it somewhere. Vanquishing, now, I really like vanquishing. Poof, it's gone! Anyhow, take your pick."

Would you like me to preview whatever your new friend is hunting? (Fizzbin)

What good will that do? (Dawk)

Dawk continued behind Nazo, who slowly began to pull out his naginata. The tengu under the tent did not notice them. Nazo moved in suddenly, springing into the tent in a graceful way that Dawk did not expect at all. Nazo swung the naginata upward, ripping away the tent and exposing the face of the very frightened tengu.

It was just some old man, not any kind of monster, but Nazo's fierce movements made it clear that he didn't think so. To Nazo, this old man was a monster. A cowering monster who dropped to his knees and started to drip sweat as he begged for mercy.

"Please, please, spare me," the old man said to Nazo. "I have done you no harm!"

"You have threatened me with that nose of yours!" Nazo said. "You follow me everywhere. You rip apart people's property. I'm in the mood for a good old-fashioned vanquishing."

It was true, the old man did have a huge nose.

But that didn't make him a demon. Dawk ran between them.

"Are you sure this is the tengu who has been following you?" he asked Nazo. "It doesn't look like a tengu to me! No wings!"

"They're under his robes. That's obvious! Old trick."

"Take off my robes!" the old man cried. "You will see no wings!"

Nazo stood still and stared down at the man, trying to decide what to do next.

"I think you're very tired and hungry," Dawk said gently. "You're not thinking straight. You need to get something in your stomach. It rumbled so loud it almost ruined the play for me, and now look at you. Your actions are crying out for a snack. I'll find you an umeboshi. Come back to the castle with me."

"The castle? You live in the castle?" Nazo's attention turned away from the old man.

"My family is visiting the castle," Dawk told him. "They must have an umeboshi in there somewhere, right? It's a castle! What won't they have?"

"Perhaps you could arrange a place for me to stay," Nazo said. "Maybe he isn't the tengu, but there is one out there, hunting me down. You get me in the castle for a night, I'll be protected. He won't find me. He'll give up, go back to the mountain, bother some other yamabushi."

They walked off together, though Dawk turned and bowed to the old man, who was now back on his feet and gathering up the tent that Nazo had ravaged.

That was a very good use of psychology to diffuse a tense situation, Dawk. (Fizzbin)

I just hope the castle has a stockpile of these pickled plums, or there may be more trouble tonight. (Dawk)

The sun was beginning to go down as Dawk and Nazo entered Numata Castle.

When they came to the guards, Dawk introduced Nazo. "A guest of my family," Dawk said. "All he requires is a floor and one umeboshi. What would you suggest?"

The second guard gave Dawk directions first to the kitchen, where the umeboshi were stored, and then to an area of the castle where the monk could sleep in peace.

Is it too late for me to ask whether this is a good idea,

Dawk? Your family's reputation within the castle is on the line. This mad monk could ruin it and cost us the mission. (Fizzbin)

The guy needs a place to sleep, and he's not asking for much. He deserves at least a hard floor for all the crazy things he's been telling me about demons in the mountains. You wanted me to learn something about Japan. (Dawk)

I don't know if the ramblings of a mountain hermit are quite what I had in mind. (Fizzbin)

Dawk stopped. "How does this floor look?" he asked.

Nazo used his foot to scrape around and kick up some dust. "Not dirty enough," he said. "Maybe there's some place filthier I could sleep? I sat on that comfortable wooden seat for the length of the noh, so now I must sleep the night on the dirtiest, hardest floor I can find to even it out."

"Just lie down. I think the dirt here is exactly what you're looking for," Dawk said. He was starting to get annoyed with the monk's weird way of looking at things. "I'll go grab you an umeboshi from the kitchen."

"Just find me half a plum," Nazo said. "That'll even things out."

CHAPTER

11

The next day, Dawk and Hype woke up at the same time and went to eat breakfast with their parents.

While they ate, Dawk told his family what he'd done the day before.

"So your friend is just on the floor in some hallway?" Hype asked.

"That's what he wanted," Dawk said. "And I wouldn't exactly call him my friend."

Mom put a plate of *natto*, a sort of sticky breakfast goo, on the table. "I'm sure we could have arranged for something more comfortable for him," she said.

"He's used to it," Dawk said. "He likes it that way, really. He lives in the mountains alone, except for all the giant flying squirrels he has to fight."

"What's a flying squirrel?" Dad asked.

"And why does he need to fight them?" asked Mom. "They must be very dangerous."

A flying squirrel is a type of a rodent creature common to this era and for hundreds of years to follow. The non-flying type was well known in cities at one point, most famous for living in green areas and going up to strangers for nuts. (Fizzbin)

"That doesn't really explain what a flying squirrel is," Dad said. "Do they have claws or fangs?"

The conversation about flying squirrels went on until breakfast was done. Fizzbin worked overtime providing the family with photos from the history banks of all sorts of squirrels so they would understand better.

Mom and Dad were soon out the door to learn about shoes, wearing their own very uncomfortable wooden shoes. Dawk and Hype left together a few minutes later. They wandered the inner maze of Numata Castle until Hype found the courtyard where she was supposed to meet Komatsuhime.

"So she's going to teach you to be a samurai?" Dawk asked. "I didn't even know girls could be samurais."

"They're not samurais, they're onna-bugeisha," Hype said. "It's all in NeuroPedia. You should take a look."

Dawk shook his head. "Flying squirrels have used up my education quota for the day."

CHAPTER

12

Hype held her staff directly in front of her face and stood ready for . . . something. She wasn't quite sure what.

Attack? Praise? Adjustment? Maybe she wasn't holding the staff quite right.

I could easily transfer visuals of samurai battle stances into your NeuroCache for reference. (Fizzbin)

Thank you, but I want to learn this without cheating. (Hype)

It's not cheating. It's using the tools available to you. (Fizzbin)

Hype wasn't so sure about that. It didn't seem like cheating in the twenty-fifth century where everyone had the same access, but it sure seemed like cheating in the past.

If she was in some kind of danger, sure, bring on NeuroPedia and whatever else her home century had to offer, but it didn't seem right for now.

"Not bad," Komatsuhime said. "But there is room for improvement."

"I'm sorry," said Hype.

"There is nothing for you to feel sorry about," Komatsuhime said. "There is always room to improve anything you do. At the very least, the desire to improve might not actually improve, but it will keep you in top form."

"But why is a stance so important?" Hype asked. "Why do I need to practice standing here?"

Komatsuhime laughed. "Your stance is the most important thing you will learn," she said. "If nothing else, how you stand says whether your opponent can knock you around while he swings his own weapon. Even if you can't defeat him with offensive moves, you can still save yourself some pain with a solid defense. But also, your stance is a way of passing on a secret message, one of confidence. It is your way of telling an opponent that you are not worried by the threat of him. You hold your naginata steady, and you look him in the eyes. Works well enough for a man, but coming from a woman, it is terrifying."

Hype practiced a serious expression, but she wasn't sure it was very convincing. Komatsuhime watched her with a blank face, which didn't exactly make Hype feel very terrifying or powerful.

"But what if the opponent swings up and down instead of left and right?" Hype asked. "I don't think my stance is going to help much."

"You're getting ahead of yourself," Komatsuhime said. "Master one stance before you practice another. The only way to defeat an opponent is to defeat an opponent. Now, are you ready to spar a little? We need to get a feel for your swing."

CHAPTER

13

Dawk zoomed through the castle passages. But when he turned a corner and expected the monk to be sitting in his little spot, he was gone.

Perhaps he is not one for goodbyes. (Fizzbin)

Well, if he's gone, I don't exactly know what I'm going to do with my day. (Dawk)

Dawk wandered over to the kitchen to look for Nazo there. Servants were all around, but no monk.

A girl came up to Dawk and bowed. "Good morning, esteemed guest of Lord Sanada. Do you need assistance?" she said.

"I'm looking for a monk," Dawk said. "Armor, robes, a little smelly. Very talkative. Have you seen him? He was sleeping out in the hallway here."

"Oh, yes, he was in earlier," the girl said. "He said he needed to finish the umeboshi he ate half of last night, which he did, and then said he was going to tour the castle alone. I warned him of which direction to avoid."

"Avoid?" Dawk asked.

"Yes. The Forbidden Area. Many horrible incidents there."

I believe you know as well as I do where your friend is. (Fizzbin)

"What is the Forbidden Area?" Dawk asked.

"It's just an old storage room, but people are always reporting it as a place yokai attack them. No one knows why yokai would hang around there, though."

"That sounds like the kind of place this monk would go. Thank you, um . . ."

"Junko," the girl said. "Now, do you want me to show you where it is?" She held her head high and added, "No yokai scares me."

Dawk, can we not involve another local right now? (Fizzbin)

"Oh, that's okay," Dawk told the girl. "Just point me in the right direction. I'll find him."

Dawk hoped he hadn't caused any trouble by bringing Nazo into the castle. Nazo was unpredictable, and Dawk just didn't need the misery. There was a noise in the distance, a kind of scuffling accompanied by grunting.

OpBot audio sensors just picked up— (Fizzbin)

Weird noises? My ears picked that up, too. (Dawk)

Dawk paused to listen carefully and then followed the sounds. They were coming from a corridor to the right, so he turned there and marched through. The hallway was lined with doors, but finally he came to one that opened into a room where Nazo stood, naginata flailing around him.

Dawk stayed at the doorway and stared dumbfounded at Nazo as he swung his weapon, kicked, and did flips.

Is he practicing? (Dawk)

The OpBot flew over, circling around Nazo's

head before stopping in front of his face and hovering there while he moved around.

An analysis of his eye movements suggests that he is looking at something that isn't there. Mapping his body movements supports this. It's as if he is fighting an invisible monster. If invisible monsters existed, that is. (Fizzbin)

He doesn't notice me standing here. (Dawk)

Dawk wasn't sure what to do.

Was Nazo in some kind of monk trance? Was this training? Should he just leave him alone and come back later to check on him?

What if one of the castle guards found him in here acting like this? Would that mean that Dawk would get in big trouble?

Nazo turned and raised the naginata above his head, barreling toward Dawk in the entrance. Dawk quickly spun out of the way.

Nazo tripped over his foot and flew into the wall. Then he turned around, shook his head as if trying to wake himself up, and slumped down to the ground.

"Where did the tengu go?" he asked hazily.

Dawk stood up.

I would advise to you to proceed with caution. He still has that naginata in his hand, and he appears incoherent. As he usually does. (Fizzbin)

"Nazo, it's me," Dawk said. "It's your new friend . . . Dawk. Do you remember me from yesterday?"

Nazo looked at Dawk, confused.

"Remember me?" Dawk went on. "We were at the noh together! Um, remember? I gave you snacks! You love snacks! I bet we could go get you a snack now. I made a friend in the kitchen, and she's got a nice half of an umeboshi waiting there for you."

Nazo's face twitched, and Dawk saw that he tightened his grip on his weapon.

"Fool me once, aha, but fool me twice, no, no, no," Nazo growled. "I am not stupid, and I am not crazy. You were the tengu all along, weren't you? Taking the form of a boy, luring me into a castle, and tempting me with plums. You leave me defenseless and trusting in the night. When I am pacified to a point that you might take advantage of me, you show your true face. Bam! And now you think I am fooled because you appear to me as the boy again?"

"What are you talking about?" Dawk asked.

What is he talking about? (Dawk)

If I understand his ramblings correctly, he thinks that you are a demon who has tricked him and tried to kill him. (Fizzbin)

Really? I thought I was pretty nice to him. Did I do something offensive that I didn't know about? (Dawk)

Probably, but I don't think that's why he's upset. (Fizzbin)

Nazo began to pull himself off the ground. Dawk backed away. "Nice Nazo, nice monk," he said. "Did the plum make your stomach growly? Is that it? Or you did you need a more comfortable floor to sleep on? Whatever it is, I'll make it right. I promise."

Nazo stood up. "The only thing that will make this right is my defeat of the tengu that has been torturing me for days and nights and days and nights!" he snarled.

Dawk knew exactly what that meant and took

off down the corridor. He could hear Nazo racing behind him, babbling.

The corridor was confusing. Dawk thought he could find his way back if he was calm, but with a madman chasing him, he wasn't sure every move would be the right one.

I need you to tell me where I'm going. (Dawk)

Take the next corridor to the right and then another right at the second doorway. (Fizzbin)

Nazo was still behind him.

I don't know where you're taking me, but is there a plan for when we get there? That's what I need to know. (Dawk)

There is a plan. Have no fear. (Fizzbin)

Dawk followed Fizzbin's instructions. The OpBot was in front of him, so he focused on that as he ran. It was good to have something to look at. Running in the wooden shoes was just about the most painful thing Dawk had ever felt.

Dawk nearly couldn't stop himself fast enough when Fizzbin's directions led him to slam directly into a door. He turned around in terror to see the monk coming right at him.

Open the door, Dawk. (Fizzbin)

Dawk fumbled quickly at a latch and pulled it, but the door didn't do anything. He shook at it. Still nothing. He shoved his entire body against it.

Only when he went flying through it and tumbled to the ground did he realize that the door was covered in thin white paper that made it look solid.

That is not an efficient way to open a sliding door, Dawk. (Fizzbin)

Dawk looked up, trying to see where he was. The wall nearest him was empty except for a few weapons placed on the wall.

But then he saw motion out of the corner of his eye, and he turned. His sister and the lady of the castle were battling with long sticks.

"Dawk!" Hype yelled. "What do you think you're doing?"

But before Dawk could answer, Nazo came flying into the room. Dawk rolled out of the way. Komatsuhime shifted into a battle position.

It looked like the woman and the monk were going to crash. Dawk closed his eyes.

You should really watch this. You won't believe it. (Hype)

Even I will admit that this is quite an impressive display. (Fizzbin)

When Dawk opened his eyes, he saw Komatsuhime quickly bend over, causing Nazo to trip on top of her.

This allowed Komatsuhime to quickly jerk up and send Nazo into a back flip, sending him crashing against the wall.

Komatsuhime turned and poked her stick on the stunned monk's nose.

"I regret that I must ask you to leave this castle immediately," she said to him. "Forgive me for any rudeness."

CHAPTER

14

Nazo wasn't calm, but he wasn't stupid. He left when Komatsuhime asked him to. Guards arrived to lead him out, but Dawk didn't think they were needed. Nazo knew he had to go.

Just before he left, the monk turned to Komatsuhime and scowled. "I may live simply, but my brain is very complicated. I think about all sorts of things. Like why this tengu is welcome in your castle. Before now, I've only seen it in the open. An empty belly does not mean an empty brain. I will return with more of me."

What is he talking about? (Hype)

Sounds like a threat. (Dawk)

Komatsuhime did not flinch or show even the slightest concern. "I would say the man is mad if we hadn't had such encounters before," she told Dawk and Hype as the guards led Nazo away. "The Forbidden Area was once used for storage. Kitchen staff refused to enter it after several incidents, though it has been a while."

"You've had problems in that room before?" Hype asked.

"That depends on what you consider problems," Komatsuhime said. She smiled. "They are dealt with swiftly. More like episodes that require a calming down."

Some kind of mass hysteria, no doubt. Stories get around, and people see things they want to see. (Fizzbin)

"Did other people report the same thing as my brother's friend?" Hype asked. "And did you believe them?"

"It is not always tengu," said Komatsuhime. "There have been *azukiarai, nurikabe, nure-onna, ashiarai yashiki, o-dukuro, tsuchigumo,* at least one *nue.* Those are the ones I remember. Some kitchen staff have claimed to see *Seto Taisho*. At least one washing woman was attacked by an *akaname*. And one woman said her parents were there, which was unusual."

Dawk did his best to take that list and cross-reference with NeuroPedia, but it was a chore, and he got confused about what was what.

Was the *nure-onna* the giant skeleton or the snake lady? Which was the guy from the bathtub that liked to eat mildew? *Nurikabe* was a wall? What did that mean?

It was maddening.

How many pretend monsters does Japan have? (Dawk)

I would urge you to study the information on yokai that NeuroPedia offers. Most people only access it to help with PlayMods. (Fizzbin)

"And did you or your husband do anything about these encounters?" Hype asked.

"We directed a man to build a wall and seal off the room," Komatsuhime said. "It seemed the easiest way to get rid of what was more a nuisance than a danger. But it didn't turn out very well. *Wanyudo* attack."

That unlucky fellow lost all his limbs if that's the case. (Fizzbin)

"So he died?" asked Dawk.

"Oh, no," Komatsuhime said. "None of them ever die. They all escape, unharmed. But the terror they feel prevents them from ever going near the room again. My husband and I were the only two who would actually go to the room. We cleaned it out. We didn't see anything in there. No monsters at all."

"So do you think the monsters don't exist?" asked Hype.

"That's not really the point," Komatsuhime explained. "We do not require proof from the eyes to accept such creatures in our understanding of reality. It does not matter. They exist to explain the world, and they live their lives in our stories. That is what made these incidents so odd." She paused and then went on, "People do not see these creatures. They just know them. The creatures themselves aren't what is scary. Seeing them is."

She sighed and turned to Hype. "Enough rest and monster tales. We need to continue your training."

CHAPTER

15

Dawk crept back toward the Forbidden Area.

This is a terrible idea. I don't know what you hope to gain. (Fizzbin)

That stuff Komatsuhime was saying didn't strike you as weird? (Dawk)

It struck me as weird, yes, but a lot of things humans say strike me as weird. (Fizzbin)

It struck me as weird in a 'I wonder how the people from the future are involved in this one' way. (Dawk)

Dawk and his sister had encountered evidence of people from the future—*their* future—tampering with the past in previous trips with their parents. Making people see demons in a castle seemed exactly like the sort of thing the future visitors would do to disrupt the past.

I doubt they are behind this. There is nothing in that room, and it is an empty and forgotten place in a part of an old castle. None of it has the slightest historical importance. The only thing that has happened is that superstitious people have seen and heard things in a bout of mass hysteria. You were in that room yourself, and you saw nothing but an out-of-control monk. (Fizzbin)

Dawk was sure that the strange goings-on in the Forbidden Area had something to do with the meddlers from the future that they had met on earlier missions. He was sure of it. But he didn't have any proof, so it was probably going to be a lot of work to convince Fizzbin.

"Excuse me!" came a call from down the corridor. Dawk turned to see Junko jogging toward him. "I heard about the tengu!" she said. "Very exciting!"

"That news is getting around the castle awfully fast," Dawk said. "Hey, I have an idea. I was going to take another look at the Forbidden Area, because when it all happened, I didn't see any tengu. I just saw a screaming guy. Maybe if you came with me, we could keep each other brave and prove there's nothing spooky there?"

Are you sure this is a good idea? (Fizzbin)

I think it's a great idea. I don't think I can do this without someone from the actual era to maybe see what everyone else sees. (Dawk)

"I don't know," Junko said. "I don't want to lose my kitchen position, but I would rather hunt for yokai."

"It would only take a couple minutes, right?" Dawk said. "We walk in, we look, nothing happens, we leave. I escort you back to the kitchen, you bring me a snack because you're nice. Simple!"

Junko smiled. "I suppose they wouldn't miss me for a couple of minutes."

Dawk turned to walk and Junko followed him. They kept a slow pace as they walked toward the Forbidden Area.

"How long have you worked in the kitchen?" Dawk asked her.

"Since I was little, and my mother brought me

to work with her. I liked the kitchen and helped my mother with her jobs. I did very well, so now I work there, too. It's not very exciting."

"Komatsuhime seems like a nice person to work for."

"She is a very gracious and brave mistress," Junko replied. She was quiet for a moment and then added, "I wish I had her skills as a warrior."

The entrance to the Forbidden Area was near. Junko stopped when she saw it. "I suppose nothing too horrible could be in that room," she said. "At worst, rats, and I see those in the kitchen now and then."

"That's right," Dawk said. "Nothing to worry about."

They paused just outside the door and then hurried in together.

Dawk looked around. It was dark but empty. There was nothing there but the brick walls. He let his muscles relax. Dawk stayed calm for roughly two seconds before something struck him in the back of the neck, and he turned to see Junko with her arm ready for another try at him.

"Hey!" Dawk said. "Why'd you hit me?"

Junko didn't answer. It was like she was in some kind of trance. Her eyes were wide open, but she was staring past Dawk.

Dawk turned and saw nothing, just the empty, dark room. Junko swiped again, and he ducked. She walked past him.

Are you scanning this room? (Dawk)

There's no invisible creature in there, if that's what you want to know. (Fizzbin)

How about a quick scan of Junko? (Dawk)

The OpBot buzzed around her. Dawk moved in front of her to see if that would stop her from moving, but she just kept on walking. She didn't notice him at all.

It does appear that there is unusual heightened activity in this girl's temporal lobe, as if it is processing something that is not here. She may be experiencing a hallucination. (Fizzbin)

Have you scanned for a NeuroNet signal in this room? I don't know how she could receive it without a neural bypass, but she kind of looks like someone who's multi-PlayModding. (Dawk)

Of course. That was the first thing I did when your friend the monk went berserk. (Fizzbin)

Junko pressed her back against a wall and sank down to the floor. Even when she was sitting down, her legs kept moving as if she were walking backward, like she was acting out a dream.

I was thinking that it must be possible for signals to be transmitted through time on different neuro-frequencies, not just the frequency we use in the twenty-fifth century. But I bet you checked for that already. (Dawk)

There was no answer.

You didn't, did you? You didn't think of that. (Dawk)

Scanning protocol would not require me to do so. (Fizzbin)

Please, just do it. (Dawk)

Dawk waited patiently, basking in the satisfaction of having caught Fizzbin in a mistake. For the NeuroNet to be picked up, a temporal signal would have to be sent back for the time travelers to connect with.

NeuroNet transmissions worked like the old radio waves did around the twentieth century, so it seemed possible to Dawk that people on a

NeuroNet from the future might connect with that transmission on a different frequency from twenty-fifth-century citizens. That would make sure twenty-fifth-century citizens didn't pick up the future frequency, which Dawk couldn't imagine the future people would want to happen.

There is a signal in this room, but I don't know where or from what. (Fizzbin)

No idea? (Dawk)

None. But I would suggest that you are right. It is the source of the girl's trance. I recommend that you ease her out of the room until she is far enough from the signal that she comes out of her state. (Fizzbin)

Dawk helped Junko up. She struggled a little, but seemed too tired to resist. He helped her stumble out the door.

Safe in the hallway, she sat down across from the door, looking dazed.

"Are you okay?" Dawk asked. "Junko, are you with me? Do you understand what I'm saying? Are you okay?"

Junko looked groggy, her eyes blinking rapidly. She squinted, as if trying to focus on something inside the room, and then let out a sigh. "Where did the Seto Taisho go?" she said. "The Seto Taisho! Am I safe?"

"You're safe," Dawk said. "Come on, I'll help you get back to the kitchen."

He slung her arm over his shoulder and helped her stumble through the corridors, heading back toward the kitchen.

"I did my best to fight him off," she mumbled. "He broke apart one of the times. I stood my ground."

I guess it's not any kind of mass hysteria, huh? (Dawk)

I stand corrected. (Fizzbin)

That signal must have something to do with people going loopy in that room. (Dawk)

I have already stood corrected. Do you wish me to say it again? (Fizzbin)

No, I'm just enjoying the moment. (Dawk)

Well, now that you are the superior intellect here, you must already have accessed the history banks to read about the Seto Taisho the girl just mentioned. (Fizzbin)

No, you beat me to that. What is your processor speed, anyhow? (Dawk)

Now is not the time, Dawk. A Seto Taisho is some form of Japanese demon, like a tengu, but different in appearance. It is known for attacking kitchen staff, and its form is made up entirely of cooking utensils and other items found in a kitchen. (Fizzbin)

No wonder Junko was freaked out. (Dawk)

Dawk was almost dragging Junko along when he finally reached a bench just outside from the kitchen and eased her down on it. He went into the kitchen and found a ladle and cup, poured in some water, and dashed back to her, hardly spilling any of it.

Junko drank it down, a little too fast, but it seemed like she really needed it.

"What happened in there?" Dawk asked once she was alert.

"Did you not see the creature?" said Junko.

"I didn't see anything. I saw you flipping out about something, but I didn't see what it was," Dawk replied.

"It attacked me. It had butcher knives for hands,

but I fought it. It swiped at me, but never touched me, and I was able to push and kick it away. Then it cornered me and was upon me, but before it could do anything to hurt me, an invisible creature pulled me away from it. I don't know what. An *ashi-magari* wouldn't have saved me. It must be some other invisible yokai."

That's exactly how it feels to use a CartoMod. You're wandering around in this vReality map, but all the things that weren't there when they engineered it, like the people you're with, they don't show up in the CartoMod. It's so weird. I think there's still a lot of work to be done on CartoMods. (Dawk)

You are right about that. And you already know what this means. (Fizzbin)

I already told you that we've encountered the future time travelers again. You should learn to listen to me. (Dawk)

I do listen to you. I just require proof instead of mere human intuition. (Fizzbin)

"How do you keep track of all those yokai? How do you know all their names?" Dawk asked.

"I don't," Junko said. "If I did, I would know

what creature rescued me from the Seto Taisho, wouldn't I?"

CHAPTER

16

Hype picked at her rice and vegetables while the rest of the family gorged themselves.

"Once you move past clogs and sandals, it gets a little more interesting," Dad said as he munched on dinner.

"Like with *kutsu*, the riding boots," Mom said. "Very cute. I wish we could wear those instead of these awful *geta* that are always killing my feet."

I wondered if I might have the family's attention right now. There has been a slight change in mission that we need to go over. (Fizzbin)

Have they expanded our field of study to robes? There are lots of exciting robes I see, all around, and that would certainly help perk us up once we get through the kutsu. (Dad)

Sadly, no. However, the incident this morning with the kitchen worker and the stream in the Forbidden Area was brought to Benton's attention and, in turn, the Chancellor's. They agree that the discovery of the stream is of top importance, and we need to find out from where it originates. (Fizzbin)

Fizzbin began to give the Faradays a lecture in basic NeuroNetting, which all of the Faradays had learned when they were kids and had no interest in hearing again.

The NeuroNet originated on the computer system in the Alvarium. It contained all the data of NeuroPedia and the history banks. It also held all the vReality mods that could be accessed, all the systems through which people communicated through the Link, and all the hidden communications between IntelliBoards throughout the system and administrators and leaders. The Alvarium computer system sent out an electronic signal around the Alvarium, which people accessed through their neural bypasses. That signal allowed everyone to enjoy what the computer system had to offer.

For time traveling, a special limited signal system was set up. The computer system in the Alvarium sent a dedicated NeuroNet signal through a tiny node that was kept open for each traveler, linking the twenty-fifth century with whatever era the time traveler was visiting.

The problem is that this new signal is not coming from the twenty-fifth century, even though it is a signal that is traveling through the time vortex to be accessed in Numata Castle. (Fizzbin)

So where is it coming from? (Dad)

And why is it making people have illusions? (Dawk)

Is it the future time travelers? (Hype)

I have discussed the best course of action. It is important that we find a way to receive the temporal signal. We will then send a virtual agent through that signal's stream in order to attempt to access whatever banks are at the other end of it. In short, we'll hack into the other system. (Fizzbin)

Does that mean we will have a guest with us? (Mom)

No, Benton prefers to make use of the materials already in place, which means I am to be the virtual agent unleashed in the stream. But the particulars of the plan do not mean that I will be any less of service to your family during my mission. (Fizzbin)

Being a virtual agent sounds dangerous. Is it dangerous? (Hype)

There are precautions being taken. A backup of me will be what is sent in as a virtual agent. This will make sure that I cannot be damaged and also hopefully prevent any links to our own systems. The technical problem of how I will access the stream, though, is the more pressing issue. (Fizzbin)

You can't just hop signals? (Dad)

No. I will need a host to hold my backup. In much the same way that your neural bypass accesses a vReality PlayMod, my host will access this signal. The host's brain will allow my backup, held in a NeuroCache, to hop the data stream and enter the source in whatever era they come from. The host must be able to handle himself well in vReality situations. That is an important skill. (Fizzbin)

Do you know what the host will be? (Mom)

Dawk is the best choice. (Fizzbin)

Dawk? Really? (Hype)

Yes, though he'll need some modifications to his NeuroNet capabilities. A NeuroCache enlargement, for instance, will be required to hold my backup. And Dawk's neural bypass will be shut off temporarily so he can pick up this negative signal and enter the stream. (Fizzbin)

I get to ride the data stream to a future computer? That's great! (Dawk)

Dawk without the Link? I can't imagine it. (Hype)

I don't need the Link, Hype. I haven't entered a PlayMod in days. Mad monks and kitchen staff being attacked by fake Japanese demons are keeping me too busy! (Dawk)

Oh, my hero! (Hype)

And when are you and Dawk going to go on this virtual mission? (Mom)

After dinner, he will be pulled back to the twenty-fifth century by Benton to have his modifications. (Fizzbin)

Well, then, we'd better serve the eel so Dawk can get on his way! (Dad)

I'm pretty full. And I'm eager to save the day. Why don't we go now, Fizzbin? (Dawk)

CHAPTER

17

Dawk materialized back in Japan the following morning, when the family was eating breakfast. Mom was the first to notice that he'd returned.

"How did it go, sweetie?" she asked.

"Oh, you know. It wasn't exactly brain surgery," Dawk said.

Dawk sat down at the table to grab something to eat before he went data surfing into the future. He was starved, especially since he had skipped the eel for dinner the night before.

No time to sit. Grab a plum and get going. This

mission is more important than your stomach. (Backup Fizzbin)

What are you doing in my head? I'm off-Link now. (Dawk)

This is my backup residing in your cache. It's as functional as myself, though I am no longer available to you. It is not me, but it functions as me and should be considered me. Let's just agree that it is me for now. Later, when you come back on-Link and I can sync with your NeuroCache, it will become more a part of me and I will become a whole network of the data from me, myself, and this, my backup. Simple. (Backup Fizzbin)

That's not simple. That's very confusing. It's you, but it's not you? (Dawk)

If you don't understand how data is backed up and duplicated, this is not a good time for me to explain it. (Backup Fizzbin)

Sounds like the real you. (Dawk)

Dawk sighed. The one perk of being off-Link was suddenly gone. He'd probably have to listen to Backup Fizzbin nonstop in his head now.

"Fizzbin wants to know if the backup is working properly," Dad said.

"If he means is his backup even more annoying than the real thing, yes, it is."

"Dawk, be polite to Fizzbin!" Mom said, and then whispered, "You never know what gets back to the Chancellor."

"Oh, Fizzbin wanted me to pass on some instructions," Hype said. "He said that you will have the OpBot in the room with you so that he can monitor you and call on one of us to help you if something goes wrong."

"What could go wrong?" Dawk asked. "And does my Fizzbin know that? If Fizzbin thought of it after he backed up into my NeuroCache, is it in the backup? Do I have to let my Fizzbin know that the real Fizzbin said that?"

Hype patted her brother on the back. "Wow, I know that one Fizzbin gets you crazy," she said, "but I didn't expect that two would make it worse for you. What's the other Fizzbin like?"

"He's like Fizzbin," Dawk said. He paused and added, "Actually, he's a little more impatient."

"What do you think they'll do with the other Fizzbin when you're done with him?" Hype asked.

"Probably sync them up," Dawk said, "and then only one will survive. The original."

"Well, that's creepy."

"No, creepy is having one of them in your head and your head alone. He's actually talking to me right now, but I'm ignoring him while I eat."

Dawk continued to shove bits of fruit into his mouth while he watched his sister leave for her special training.

Perhaps you are fueled up enough on pears that we can get moving? (Backup Fizzbin)

Dawk did not respond. He just moved on to eating plums. He didn't want to enter mysterious temporal data streams on an empty stomach, and he didn't want the voice in his head to sour his stomach so soon.

CHAPTER 18

When Hype arrived in the training chambers, Komatsuhime was standing in full armor, gripping two naginatas. Hype studied the curved blade at the end of the poles and shivered.

"I don't know about that," Hype said. "Isn't it too much for a beginner?"

"I am the only one of the two of us who really needs to worry about getting hurt," Komatsuhime said. "You don't have the control I do. That is why I am wearing my armor. And while your logical brain tells you I will be careful to keep you safe, in the heat of the moment, you will react as if you are truly in danger, and then you will feel what it is actually like in battle."

"Is that important?"

"It is if you expect to be prepared for battle," Komatsuhime replied.

Do I really need to be prepared for battle? (Hype)

You're the one who wanted to become Komatsuhime's understudy. This is serious business. She's not here to play around. You were very excited for bruises before. (Fizzbin)

I don't want to lose an eye or an arm, though. I need those! (Hype)

To back out now would be rude to Komatsuhime. Just have your parents stand by with bandages. (Fizzbin)

Thanks for the vote of confidence. (Hype)

Komatsuhime handed a naginata over to Hype. "Hold it for a moment," Komatsuhime said. "Hold it as still as you can. Feel it. Let the weight of it sink into your arm, so that you meet it halfway and it becomes an extension of your limbs."

Hype tried to do as Komatsuhime said, but it was difficult. She couldn't figure out how to convince herself that a pointy stick was a part of her body.

"You cannot do it, can you?" Komatsuhime said.

"I'm trying," Hype said.

"I couldn't do it when I was starting out, either."

"When did you start out?" Hype asked.

"I was a very small child. The last thing I was interested in was learning the way of the onna-bugeisha. I liked running around trying to catch insects much more."

"What made you change your mind?"

"The tales of the great warrior women past," Komatsuhime told her.

"Tell me about them," Hype said.

Komatsuhime smiled. "Tomoe Gozen, who lived four hundred or so years ago, and took on thirty men without flinching. Or Empress Jingu, alive more than a millennium ago, who led armies to conquer the Three Kingdoms of Korea. And there were others. They all convinced me that I could do more than spend my days managing my future husband's property, the common fate of young girls who do not become nuns."

Komatsuhime smiled again at this and put her face down, as if she were a little embarrassed. "Let's spar," she said. "Gently for now. You follow my lead in intensity of blows. I will not rush you."

Hype held up her weapon, and Komatsuhime tapped it slightly. Hype responded as if ready to block a blow.

Komatsuhime eased her naginata from the other direction, and Hype followed instinctively with her own naginata.

It was play-fighting, Hype understood.

"When we are in training as children," Komatsuhime said, "we are taught to hold back our feelings and not let them interfere with our strategy. When your mind is cleared of clutter, it gives you the opportunity not only to win small victories that lead up to a larger one, but also to see what lies ahead in front of you. It allows for true planning, so that you get what you want."

Komatsuhime twirled her naginata down clockwise. She began to bring it up in the same direction, but reversed it and raised it the other way. Hype had prepared for the move that Komatsuhime had started, but she adjusted quickly and crashed her naginata into Komatsuhime's.

"That is a small victory," Komatsuhime said, "but it shows that you have it in you to build to the larger one. And then onward."

Komatsuhime's naginata breezed toward Hype, who pushed it aside with her own.

It was easy, but Hype was worried that she was boring Komatsuhime.

The worst thing Hype could think of doing would be to bore the older woman. It was a pretty big honor that the lady of the castle, an accomplished warrior, had taken this visiting foreign girl under her wing.

Maybe, Hype thought, she should do something to prove she was worthy of being Komatsuhime's choice.

Surprise her with a move.

That was it!

She thought about scanning through samurai PlayMod scenarios to find a clever one, but decided against it. This would have to be her own if it was going to mean anything.

Komatsuhime shoved her naginata toward Hype. Hype didn't move. She just stood in place, pushing her own pole back at Komatsuhime, making it circle quickly around Komatsuhime's pole and then, at the right moment, pulling it back.

The curved blade of Hype's hooked quickly onto Komatsuhime's. That allowed Hype to pull the naginata out from the warrior's hands and fling it against the wall.

Komatsuhime stood still for a moment, and then her shoulders shook slightly as her lips formed a grin. She laughed.

"Thank you for showing mercy to your teacher," Komatsuhime said. "And accept that I will remember that trick."

Hype was speechless and thrilled. But before she could think about what to do next, two guards burst into the room.

Komatsuhime turned to them quickly. "I've asked you not to interrupt my training!" she barked at them.

"Forgive us, but it is an emergency," said one of the guards.

"The castle is under attack! An angry mob is demanding you give it the tengu you are hiding!" said the other.

"Perhaps this will be your first training during action," Komatsuhime said to Hype as she grabbed her hand and led her out of the room.

CHAPTER

19

Dawk licked his plum-sticky fingers carefully as he walked through the castle corridors with the OpBot buzzing next to him.

So when I go in there, I should just stand around? (Dawk)

The signal should find you easily enough. (Backup Fizzbin)

Am I going to pass out or go crazy or anything like that? (Dawk)

You might be able to maintain the same awareness as you would if you were in a PlayMod. It really depends on the effect the signal has on being received directly into your frontal lobe. We shall see. (Backup Fizzbin)

And the real Fizzbin knows the plan? (Dawk)

I am the real Fizzbin. (Backup Fizzbin)

Dawk stopped at the entrance to the Forbidden Area and peered in.

"Hello, Dawkins Faraday!" came a voice from down the hall. It was Junko. Dawk waved to her.

She shouldn't be here. What if something goes wrong? (Dawk)

Actually, she may be helpful. If something does go wrong, she might be able to speed along help while the OpBot stays to make a visual record of any problem. Ask her to stay with you, though outside the room where the signal will not reach her. (Backup Fizzbin)

"You caught me!" Dawk laughed.

"You were stealing?" Junko asked.

"No," Dawk said. "Just joking. Never mind. Actually, it's good you screamed over at me, because you can help me out. I'm going to enter the Forbidden Area, and it would be really helpful if I had an actual human being—um, if I had someone to watch me while I'm in there."

"But it's dangerous in there! The Seto Taisho could come back!"

A Seto Taisho wouldn't terrorize you, since you are not a kitchen worker. (Backup Fizzbin)

"I'm safe from Seto Taisho, since I don't work in a kitchen. So that's really good, right?"

"I've heard that other yokai have been seen in there!"

"That's actually very good news to someone like me," Dawk said, "because I'm a . . . monster hunter."

Junko gasped. "That's exciting! Have you ever caught one?"

"No . . . I'm . . . not at that level yet. I'm still at the chasing-them-away part of the job, and I'm working my way up to catching one. That's why I'm here. Whatever's in that room, I'm going to chase it out."

"Are you sure?" Junko asked.

"I'm trying to be, yes," Dawk said, "and that's why I need your help. Just sit out here and watch to make sure nothing creeps up behind me."

"Yes. I can do that," Junko said. She slunk back

against the wall opposite the doorway and waved as Dawk started to enter.

"And don't forget. Whatever you do, do not enter this room," he said, walking in.

Almost immediately, it felt like a sledgehammer was whacking him on the side of the head. Dawk staggered forward. The room seemed to be moving.

Do you feel anything? (Backup Fizzbin)

Yeah, but I can't describe it. It hurts. I don't like it. Is the room moving? (Dawk)

Your brain is confused. It can't tell the difference between the information it is getting through the temporal feed and the information your eyes record. A neural bypass filters a signal into the appropriate parts of your brain, but something that can access the visual center of your brain directly is likely to confuse you like this. (Backup Fizzbin)

So is the room moving or isn't it? (Dawk)

As far as your brain is concerned, it is. (Backup Fizzbin)

Dawk turned around clumsily to look out the doorway. One moment he could see Junko, the next he couldn't.

I don't know what to do. (Dawk)

My advice is to close your eyes and stop the optical information intake. This way your lobe can get used to the information in the feed. Then treat it like any other vReality Mod. (Backup Fizzbin)

Backup Fizzbin was right. The way the signal was entering Dawk's brain was different, and that was confusing him, but the key was the same as with a neural bypass—compartmentalize. That was part of his twenty-fifth-century meditation training.

Put the temporal signal in a box in his brain. Control it.

With his eyes closed, Dawk could still see the room, but it wasn't the real one. It was the virtual one that the signal was sending from the future. He walked over to the door and looked down the corridor.

Junko was nowhere to be seen, of course, since she hadn't been programmed in, but the castle was all there, ready to be explored. But where should he go? Did it matter? Was he even here to explore? What could be seen in this modified version of reality that couldn't be seen in the real castle?

And where was Backup Fizzbin?

Here I am. (Backup Fizzbin)

Dawk turned and gasped. He was facing a little kid—a tiny, little bald kid. The kid was in traditional Japanese clothing, but had only one huge eye at the center of his face.

What is that? (Dawk)

It is an avatar I am using so that you might perceive me in a physical way. A little more time and I could make my own avatar, something more familiar to you. Perhaps I could appear to you as Hype? (Backup Fizzbin)

That would be a little creepy, actually. A lot worse than the one-eyed kid. (Dawk)

It's a yokai called hitotsume-kozo, and it's very interesting. (Backup Fizzbin)

The *hitotsume-kozo* avatar Backup Fizzbin had chosen looked both ridiculous and creepy. Dawk didn't know if he was going to burst into uncontrollable laughter or be sick to his stomach.

Would you like me to tell you more about this yokai to pass the time? (Backup Fizzbin)

Dawk didn't answer. He was too busy ducking and avoiding a creature that swooped over and past him. He looked up and saw a giant black bird with huge claws near the ceiling of the Forbidden Area. It turned around and revealed the face of a hairy—and pretty angry-looking—black dog, complete with growls, fangs, and spit.

What is that? (Dawk)

A kind of tengu known as a karasu-tengu*. It's dangerous for all the obvious reasons, like its deadly claws. Fangs. It also has the ability to possess the body of the human it stalks. (Backup Fizzbin)*

The *karasu-tengu* stared at Dawk.

Can a hitotsume-kozo *beat him in a fight? (Dawk)*

Oh, I doubt it. (Backup Fizzbin)

Can he actually possess one of us? This is vReality. Can he do that in vReality? (Dawk)

It would take some very sophisticated vReality programming to commandeer your perceptions to that degree and, in fact, control you. Of course, if our theories are correct, then this signal comes from an advanced human race sometime in the future, so maybe they can do that. One hopes for astounding scientific advances like that in the future. (Backup Fizzbin)

The *karasu-tengu*, upside down on the ceiling,

inched slowly toward Dawk and Backup Fizzbin. Its eyes were ablaze. It looked happy.

Suddenly it disappeared.

Oh, yes, one more thing—it has the ability to teleport. (Backup Fizzbin)

Dawk felt something next to him and turned to see the *karasu-tengu* right on top of him, wings outstretched and lunging straight for his head with its mouth open ready to bite it off and swallow it down whole.

Everything went black.

CHAPTER 20

Hype followed Komatsuhime and the guards
through the winding paths of Numata Castle, past
all the check-in points, and finally back to the moat.
There, she saw a mob of hundreds being held back
by a few guards.

Hype scanned the crowd. Men and women
in various kinds of robes and armor, most of
them shaking some sort of weapon, yelled up at
Komatsuhime.

"Give us the tengu!"

"Tengu lover!"

"No tea with tengu!"

Hype spied Dawk's weird monk friend, Nazo, at the front of the crowd and figured that the men in the crowd must be monks since they were dressed a lot like Nazo. There were plenty of women, too, and they didn't look any happier than the guys.

"Ready your stance, Hypatia," Komatsuhime whispered. Then she walked out on the small drawbridge that laid across the moat and said nothing, just stared at the crowd that stood on the other side of it, sizing them up.

She held up her naginata and waited for the crowd to quiet. "What is your business at Numata Castle?" Komatsuhime asked once it was silent.

"You know our business," Nazo called. "I told you that I would be back. I want that tengu that you protect. He may prance around like a boy, but I know, I know!"

"The boy who stays in the castle is no tengu, monk. And I am not protecting one. Besides, a tengu comes and goes however a tengu wishes to. I have no say whether one leaps into my castle or out of it."

"There she goes!" Nazo yelled. "You see, my brothers and sisters? She admits to the tengu being in her castle without actually saying it in clear words! Typical dishonesty. Right then and there, she admitted that the tengu leaps in and out of her castle!"

There were murmurs of "tengu lover" through the crowd.

"And what are my choices in this matter?" Komatsuhime asked. "Am I to deliver a tengu that does not exist to you, or do I allow you to storm the castle in search of it?"

Seems like it would be a lot easier if Komatsuhime said that there wasn't any tengu in here and that Dawk's friend was just pretty crazy. (Hype)

That's the problem exactly, I'm afraid. Whether the monk is crazy isn't the point at all. You see, Komatsuhime did not see a tengu, but her personal spiritual beliefs will include the existence of a tengu. She cannot know for sure that a tengu is in Numata Castle, and she can't say for sure that it is not. (Fizzbin)

Komatsuhime was so calm and seemed so smart. It was odd to Hype that a woman like that would actually believe in monsters and spirits and demons. Of course she did, since she was a woman of Medieval Japan, and of course Hype should have known that all along, but Komatsuhime was different from other people whom Hype had met in the past. Komatsuhime seemed modern.

"Only yamabushi have the powers to deal with tengu properly," Nazo said. "Let us go to the boy. We'll take care of him." He motioned to a wrinkled, grimacing woman with wild silver hair next to him. "This is Chiyoye. She and I do this sort of thing together all the time."

"We have it all sorted out. We're quite good at it," Chiyoye said.

"You are definitely experts at storming castles with mobs and acting rude," Komatsuhime said. "Even if I was actively seeking a yamabushi couple to tangle with a tengu in Numata Castle, why would I ever ask you?"

"We're really quite skilled at battling tengu, you see," Chiyoye said. "And Nazo is not as bad as he seems. He just does not get out of the mountains much."

Nazo shushed her. Then he turned to Komatsuhime. "Do you think all of us came down from the mountain to be turned away?" he asked. "You didn't even think I knew so many others. You thought, here's a hermit, who does he know anyhow? If he comes back, he comes back alone! Well, I know Chiyoye, and I know my brothers and sisters, and we demand entry now! Give us the boy!"

"I'm sorry," Komatsuhime said. "I cannot give you the boy, so please return to your mountain." Then she turned away and began walking toward the castle.

Hype wasn't sure what she was supposed to be doing.

Should she follow Komatsuhime? Keep her stance? Scare away the crowd with her stare?

I would suggest retreating from your current position. (Fizzbin)

I think my body is actually frozen. (Hype)

Then Nazo raised his naginata. When he did, everyone in the crowd raised their weapons and began to move forward. Nazo and Chiyoye led the pack, naginatas ready to strike.

Finally, Hype's body moved. She swiped her naginata in front of Nazo and Chiyoye, blocking them from entry on the drawbridge. Guards rushed to stand behind her and back her up, but allowed her, as Komatsuhime's student, to take the lead in the defense.

"You heard what Komatsuhime said!" Hype yelled.

"Who are you?" Nazo said. "Just some little girl pretending to be a big warrior, trying to protect her yokai brother."

Nazo and Chiyoye began to swing their naginatas toward Hype. She bowed down, ducking underneath the paths of the weapons being swung at her, but then shoved her naginata up. That movement locked the other two naginatas around hers when they swung back.

Hype jolted her weapon upward as she stood, pulling the naginatas out of the grasps of Nazo and Chiyoye and into the air behind them. The weapons plummeted down into the moat.

"Sometimes you need to step out of the classroom to do your best," Komatsuhime said.

Hype turned. She estimated nearly a hundred castle guards had joined Komatsuhime and were standing behind her.

"Now we can battle here, or you can all go back to your mountain!" Komatsuhime called out. "You see that your leader can't even stand up against my young student. Are the rest of you up to it, with all of the forces of Numata Castle standing behind her?"

There was a pause, and then the entire crowd lowered their weapons.

"Now if you could please choose another spokesman, we can talk about this situation calmly," Komatsuhime told the crowd.

There was a disturbance in the back of the crowd, and Hype watched one man push through. When he got closer, she could see that he was not a monk.

"Shinobu," Komatsuhime said.

"Komatsuhime," he said, bowing his head. "Forgive my intrusion on this riot."

"Not at all, Shinobu," she said. "It was just ending. Is something wrong?"

"Trouble in town, in the merchant district. A beast is on the rampage. It has torn apart stalls, broken through stores."

"Tengu? Tengu?" Nazo screamed in Shinobu's face.

"Yes. That is what some claim," Shinobu said calmly.

Nazo turned to face the crowd he had brought down from the mountain. "Brothers and sisters!" he called. "To town, to town, to tangle with tengu!"

The crowd cheered, and the hundreds of them began rumbling away together from Numata Castle, leaving Hype, Komatsuhime, Shinobu, and all the guards standing there.

"Shall we follow?" Komatsuhime said. "They'll do more damage to the castle town than any tengu."

CHAPTER

21

Dawk felt like he was still alive. And he felt like he still had a head. He just couldn't see it. Or anything else.

Open your eyes. (Backup Fizzbin)

That was it. His eyes were closed. In the vReality and in real life. Dawk did not like the *karasu-tengu* at all and did not like this vReality mod at all, and maybe it would simpler if he just could open his real eyes in the real castle and let Backup Fizzbin do his job in the vReality stream.

Dawk could just wait for him in the room. That

was possible, right? He'd just talk with Junko to pass the time. A perfect plan.

Dawk, you need to open your eyes so you can navigate this vReality. (Backup Fizzbin)

Dawk let himself look into the vReality. He was no longer in a little room in the castle. Now he was near the edge of a forest, near a two-story wooden house. Dawk felt suddenly cold, and he realized it was because he was lying in snow. He was still in his Japanese clothes and Backup Fizzbin was still the weird one-eyed kid, but he was pretty sure they weren't in Japan anymore.

Why are we in the snow? Where's the castle? (Dawk)

I found a security hole in the system and was able to shoot out of that vReality stream and into another just in time. (Backup Fizzbin)

You what? (Dawk)

I theorized that the stream in Numata Castle would be contained in the same computer system as other signals being sent out to other eras, and my theory seems correct. This is a different vReality on the same system being sent who knows where or when. And where there are two, there are probably many. I can use them to work our way further into this system. Hopefully we will get to the source of the signal's origin, or at least its data center. (Backup Fizzbin)

There was a scream. It seemed like it had come from the house.

Should I go see who made that noise? (Dawk)

Do whatever you need to do to pass your time while we are here. I'll let you know if I need you. (Backup Fizzbin)

Dawk ran over, being careful to not slip in the snow. Another scream came out of the house. When Dawk peered in the window, he saw two young girls who wore long dresses and had scarves on their heads. They were being chased around by swarms of little black creatures with horns and tails. The poor girls were contorting and screeching each time one of the little monsters descended on them.

I don't think I know how to save them from those things. What are they, anyhow? (Dawk)

Whatever time period and geographical location this second signal is streamed, I imagine those creatures are part of a superstition native to them, just as the various yokai were native to Japan of 1595. (Backup Fizzbin)

And do you have any idea when or where that is? (Dawk)

I'm working on another security hole to get us out of this vReality and further into the system. (Backup Fizzbin)

Dawk couldn't watch the girls anymore. It was just weird and creepy, and he couldn't do anything for them. And, he thought, as a time traveler, maybe he wasn't supposed to anyhow.

Data reveals that this is transmitting to 1692, somewhere in Massachusetts, the Americas. Now prepare yourself for the next security hole, which I date sometime near the beginning of the twenty-first century in the urban center of Sydney, on the continent of Australia. (Backup Fizzbin)

This time Dawk's eyes were open, but he hardly noticed the change in vReality. He suddenly found himself next to Backup Fizzbin in a dark room. Someone was asleep in a bed next to a window.

What happens if they wake up? (Dawk)

Eyes open, yawning occurs. Really, Dawk, this is basic stuff, and I am busy with the next security hole. (Backup Fizzbin)

Dawk slumped against a wall and waited. From what he could see in the dim light, beds sure had changed over the centuries. So had light. In the twenty-first century, it apparently came in through windows like laser beams.

Wait. That didn't seem right.

Dawk watched as the beam surrounded the person in bed and lifted them up into the air.

What's that beam doing? (Dawk)

It is doing whatever it is designed to do in this vReality signal to people of the era it is aimed at. (Backup Fizzbin)

Big help. (Dawk)

The sleeping person, now engulfed in the beam, inched up and then straight out the window. Dawk scooted forward to try to figure out where the beam was coming from. Outside the window was a giant disc-shaped hunk of shiny silver metal with colored lights on the bottom portion. It was pulling the sleeper straight to it.

That was pretty weird.

Dawk didn't have too much time to absorb the sight. Once again, and this time with no warning from Backup Fizzbin, the vReality scenario changed to another forest. This time, it was dark. Very dark. Warm. And they were right in the middle of it.

Backup Fizzbin stayed still. Dawk listened to the sounds of the vReality woods. There were the chirps of insects, the sound of branches and leaves in the breeze.

And something stomping toward them.

Someone's coming. Fast. (Dawk)

Then I will try to get us out of here faster. (Backup Fizzbin)

Now Dawk heard flapping. Huge wings, it sounded like. It reminded him of the dragon he and Hype had seen on their mission to ancient Rome.

Dawk crouched near a tree as the noise got louder, pulling Backup Fizzbin back with him.

Do you know when and where we are? (Dawk)

A region known as New Jersey, in the year 1978. (Backup Fizzbin)

In the dark distance, the running feet came closer, and in the split second that it took the person to pass Dawk, he could see it was a boy right around his own age.

Then Dawk saw what was following the kid. It was bigger than a man, and did look very much like a dragon, a scaly reptile with a long neck. But it had huge horns and fangs, and its body was covered with fur. Its wings were flapping heavily, but its feet were on the ground running, too.

I feel like I should help that guy. (Dawk)

No time. (Backup Fizzbin)

And once again the woods faded around them, but this time, they didn't enter a new scenario.

Nothing.

There was nothing anywhere. Dawk couldn't see Backup Fizzbin's avatar. He looked for his own feet, his hands, but he couldn't see those either.

He didn't feel anything.

We're there, but I only have a moment. (Backup Fizzbin)

We're where? (Dawk)

At the core of the other system. (Backup Fizzbin)

What now? (Dawk)

A race against security. (Backup Fizzbin)

Someone's after you? The time travelers? (Dawk)

Whoever owns the system will be if you don't allow

me to channel all my resources into copying data into your NeuroCache right now. (Backup Fizzbin)

Um. Okay. Go ahead. (Dawk)

Dawk patiently waited in the nothingness. After all, there was nothing to do in the nothingness.

Don't panic. (Backup Fizzbin)

What? (Dawk)

Then things happened quickly. Dawk saw split seconds of the New Jersey forest, the Sydney apartment, and the house in Massachusetts before finally returning to the Forbidden Area in Numata Castle. It felt like freefalling.

Lie down on your side and roll toward the door. (Backup Fizzbin)

What? (Dawk)

On your side. To the door. Slowly. Don't look around. Don't listen. Don't feel. Just roll. (Backup Fizzbin)

Dawk did exactly what Backup Fizzbin told him to. He kept rolling even though he was pretty sure there was some kind of vReality monster doing its best to try to terrorize him.

But something stopped him. He couldn't roll anymore. He was stuck. He pushed, but he couldn't move. Then he felt a force down on his body, pulling him over and up.

Some kind of tengu. It had to be.

He looked up, trying to focus his eyes, and saw Junko dragging him out of the Forbidden Area. He was out of the signal's reach.

CHAPTER 22

The huge mob had swarmed into the castle town.

Hype tagged along with Komatsuhime, Shinobu, and all the guards as they worked to find the tengu and keep the crowd of monks under control. Citizens stepped out of their homes to see what all the noise was about.

Nazo's crowd screaming about tengu coming to get them all wasn't keeping anyone calm. Some men, determined to protect their families, came out with weapons and joined the chaos.

"Do you really think there is a tengu on the loose?" Hype asked Komatsuhime.

"Anything is possible," the older woman said, "but that's not really important. What is of concern to me is that something is causing trouble in Numata Town and we have a mob of mountain hermits combing the paths of it in order to correct it. They believe it is a tengu and they dealing with it as they would a tengu, so it might as well be a tengu. And we need to find out what happened."

Tengu really do not exist, right? (Hype)

I cannot guarantee that visitors from the future have not fabricated some kind of robot tengu that is currently on some rampage somewhere in the castle town. But real tengu do not exist. (Fizzbin)

As the crowd spread, Hype found it harder to keep track of, and even more difficult to keep an eye out for, what had ripped apart stores in the merchants' district. There were plenty of merchants affected by the rampage, though, and Hype kept pace alongside Komatsuhime looking into each one they came upon.

"Do not fear, citizen," Komatsuhime would say

in a soothing tone to any merchant who came up to her, "we are on the hunt for the culprit."

At each store, Hype saw the wrecked counters and merchandise, doors ripped off their hinges, shredded paper windows fluttering in the breeze, cracks in walls. Every store was a mess.

Some merchants who had seen the creature described it, and it sounded like Nazo's description of a tengu—huge nose, hairy, in bare feet and rags. No wings, though.

One man claimed it was a monster called a *satori,* which looked a bit like an ape. Komatsuhime told Hype that a *satori* could read minds, so if it was a *satori,* that explained why they couldn't find it.

Someone else was sure it was a yokai called an *otoroshi,* which was like a bunch of animals mixed together. They were very, very hairy, though it turned out that the creature rampaging through Numata Town did not have tusks like *otoroshi* were supposed to.

Still another man insisted that the attacker was an ape creature called a *hihi,* but without the signature silver fur.

"Perhaps it's just a hulking, bearded, madman," Komatsuhime said.

But they couldn't find it, whatever it was. Any outburst they investigated turned out to be neither a tengu nor a *satori,* nor even an *otoroshi* or a *hihi,* but one of the monks from the mountains making trouble.

"I'm almost convinced that nothing caused all that damage," Hype said. "People are everywhere. There is no part of this town that isn't filled with someone chasing the tengu, or whatever it is, and no one has found anything. Don't you think if something were really here, someone would have seen it by now?"

"Not if it doesn't want to be seen," Komatsuhime said.

There was a loud, horrible screech near a rice cake shop, and Komatsuhime led Shinobu and the other guards toward the noise. Hype followed behind them, more cautiously.

She didn't want to admit it, but she was afraid.

As she got closer, she saw several of the guards holding apart Chiyoye, Nazo, and a man Hype assumed was the shop owner. The awful screaming noise was coming from Chiyoye, who was twisting and contorting in a guard's grasp, trying to claw and punch him. There were bits of rice cake everywhere, and the rice cake shop owner looked like he was going to pummel Nazo.

"You must pay for that rice cake!" screamed the shop owner.

"All I ask is one rice cake for the price of protection against a tengu, that's all!" said Nazo.

"You aren't protecting me from a tengu!" the shop owner yelled. "You aren't protecting me from anything! You're just trying to steal a rice cake by claiming you have earned it!"

It was all too much for Hype. She slipped around the corner and leaned back on the wall of the shop, next to a window.

There was a rustling noise inside the shop, but it was hard to hear over Nazo, the shop owner, and Chiyoye. Hype stuck her ear close to the paper window at the back end of the building and heard some shuffling and breathing.

Someone's in there. (Hype)

I could have an OpBot sent to go in and survey the shop for you. For safety's sake. (Fizzbin)

I have my naginata. Komatsuhime is here. And all the guards. I'm not worried about my safety. I'm more worried that I'll insult the shop owner by entering his business without being invited or something like that. (Hype)

I find nothing in the social section of the history banks. You're fine to enter. (Fizzbin)

Hype went back to the front of the store. Nazo and Chiyoye were still screaming. "While you are holding me and worrying about scattered rice cakes, there is a tengu on the loose!" Nazo yelled.

Hype tapped Komatsuhime on the shoulder and motioned that she was headed inside the shop. Komatsuhime nodded solemnly and then turned her attention back to Nazo.

Inside the shop, Hype looked around for a way to the back, where she had heard the noise. She spotted a sliding door at the other end of the room and, opening it, stepped into a smaller, dark room that was piled with sacks of rice and other ingredients, pots, and pans. A storage room.

She could hear someone breathing heavily. Hype headed toward the noise. She gripped her naginata tightly and moved it to a position that would let her be ready for anything.

She heard a grunt and turned to her right, finding eyes staring right at her. She could just make out the face of the frightened creature. Deep, furry brow. Hair all over. Huge nose. Wide mouth.

Hype gasped. She knew that face.

It was the Neanderthal they had lost in the time transfer, the one who she worried was doomed to become a temporal ghost.

Here he was, not a temporal ghost at all, but a scared caveman being mistaken for a Japanese demon.

Hype walked forward and stepped on something. She looked down. Kitchen utensils, a pile of them, were strewn all over the floor.

"Are you looking for your spork?" Hype asked. "You are, aren't you?"

The Neanderthal frowned. Hype bent down and found a wooden spoon. She picked it up and showed to him. The Neanderthal watched and muttered, then turned his head, gesturing to Hype to take the spoon away.

She grabbed a little wooden paddle and waved it playfully. The Neanderthal peeked out and made a noise like his stomach hurt.

I think he wants his spork. (Hype)

Why would he look for his spork? (Fizzbin)

Maybe he only likes shiny white things. Maybe he thought it was magic or something, and it can bring him back home. I don't know. Can't you compute all the possibilities or something? (Hype)

Technically, but in order to do so I would have to have more data about the Neanderthals. (Fizzbin)

Then I think we'd better go with my idea. He wants his spork. I think our best bet is to get a fix on him and transport him away. (Hype)

You know that cannot be done without at least one other neural bypass in the room to help isolate his position. (Fizzbin)

Then plan B is that I need to get him out of this store and back to the castle, where Mom and Dad are. Then we can help Benton get a fix on him. I'm just not sure how to get him back to the castle. I think he trusts me because

I'm familiar, but he might be too scared to just follow me outside, especially with all the shouting. (Hype)

Well, a spork would be the best way to lure him out, but obviously you don't have one handy. (Fizzbin)

Can you get me one? Get me his! Get me the spork we brought back! Send it back to me right now, and I'll use that! (Hype)

I sent in a request for you, but received an immediate response of 'no.' The spork has already been handed over to the Temporal Anomaly Team, and it can't be released without a direct hearing involving the Chancellor and full council. That spork is untouchable. (Fizzbin)

That's ridiculous! It's just some dumb spork! What do they need it for? (Hype)

They are sticklers for rules. (Fizzbin)

Here's another idea. Make a time-travel request for me to Benton. I need to get to another era so I can grab another spork and use that one to lure this guy back to the castle. It wouldn't take long at all. Can you do that? (Hype)

My concern is that's a ridiculous suggestion and a waste of resources. I'm just trying to solve a temporal problem from getting worse. Neanderthal on the loose in

1595 Japan? I could request a team be sent to recover him. (Fizzbin)

He'll probably struggle, right? I can explain the Neanderthal away to Komatsuhime, but I don't think I could explain a recovery team. (Hype)

Very well. One moment . . . you have a go. Benton will get a fix on you right . . . now. (Fizzbin)

Hype felt time break down around her and saw the scared Neanderthal in the corner fade away with the rest of the room. Benton and the twenty-fifth century appeared around her.

Time for a spork hunt.

CHAPTER 23

As soon as Dawk got out of the vReality stream, the first thing he did was thank Junko for dragging him out.

"No need," she said. "You helped me before. It's the same thing."

Still, he felt like he owed her something. After all, he was from the future. He was always having adventures, even while his parents were stuck doing the dumb shoe studies. He was used to all that stuff. She wasn't. She had already had one scary encounter with the vReality stream. She didn't have to risk having another frightening experience just to help Dawk. She could have just gone and gotten someone else to come.

Dawk thought about what he could do to pay her back, and he was still considering ideas when he materialized back into Benton's lab in the twenty-fifth century to have his neural bypass reactivated.

"There's someone here I think you'd like to say hello to," Benton said and led him into another room.

Hype was standing there, getting her Visual Cortex Shell adjusted.

"You're here?" Dawk said, smiling.

"Want to go to the twentieth century with me and grab a spork somewhere?" Hype asked.

"What?"

"It's so complicated, but everyone's been looking for that tengu, right? Well, I found him. In a rice cake shop. He's not a monster or a demon at all. It's the Neanderthal! Our Neanderthal! Spork man! Remember? I've got to lure him back to the castle so I can triangulate with Mom and Dad, and Benton can get him out of there, but I needed to find some way to get him out of the shop where he's hiding. So I thought to myself, 'Spork!' Perfect, right? Spork! So I'm going to go find one."

Dawk shook his head, trying to catch up. "And you've got time for this?"

"I'm going to drop her back half a minute after I scooped her out," Benton said. "I can do the same with you, just back at the castle, and you'll meet up with your parents and be waiting when she shows up with the spork and the caveman."

"I'm in," Dawk said.

CHAPTER

24

The place was called a mall.

Benton had transported Dawk and Hype, along with an OpBot, to the year 1982, in a region of the United States called Ohio, to a place called a mall.

He had given them strict instructions to get in and out as quickly as possible. But that was easy for Benton to say. For one thing, he had no clue how difficult it was to actually find a place with sporks available. Dawk and Hype looked all over the mall. They had found plastic forks and spoons and knives and straws, but no sporks.

For another thing, the mall was an exotic wonderland of strange food smells, flashy clothing, bright colors, and booming music—and people, lots of people—that kept Dawk and Hype's senses pretty busy.

It was the exact opposite of the Alvarium's boring, beige Mall.

Fizzbin, do you think if I asked the OpBot to record some specific outfits they could be duplicated by my Visual Cortex Shell? (Hype)

Yes, that is technically possible, but the OpBot is better utilized to find a spork. (Fizzbin)

"I'm having the OpBot record some outfits for me," Hype told her brother, who was still off-Link.

Dawk pointed over to one of the stores in the mall, excited. "Dad would love that! A record store!"

"He loves looking at his records," Hype said. "Too bad he can't play them."

"Ask Fizzbin if we can bring back a record player for him to use," Dawk said.

"Even if Fizzbin said yes, we don't have any twentieth-century money to trade for the record player," Hype said.

"If we could just look at one, we could figure out how to make one for him out of junk we find in the Alvarium," Dawk said.

"Maybe Fizzbin could have the OpBot do an analysis of one after we find a spork. We could have one produced specially for him."

The OpBot has tracked down a selection of sporks at a food dispensary called The Chicken Flicker, if you would like to go there. (Fizzbin)

Where is that? (Hype)

It's right next to Pizza Plaza and across from New Wave Bop. (Fizzbin)

Is that a clothing store? (Hype)

Eyes on the spork, Hype. (Fizzbin)

They headed for The Chicken Flicker and started looking around. Napkins. Straws. Hype pulled something wrapped in plastic out of a round metal container and laughed with joy.

Should I grab a few? Just in case? (Hype)

Best not to risk it. (Fizzbin)

Hype grabbed one and motioned for Dawk to follow her out.

"Hold on there!" came a voice.

Hype turned. A lanky blond kid in a white shirt, bow tie, and straw hat was coming after them.

"The utensils are for paying customers," he said, "and I didn't see you buy anything. Not a Cock-A-Doodle Dinner. Not even a Little Clux Snack box." He eyed the spork in Hype's hand. "And you wouldn't even need that unless you got coleslaw. Are you hiding coleslaw?"

"We don't know what that is," Dawk said.

The kid frowned at them. "Wait a minute, you're those transfer students, aren't you? Are you those kids from East Germany?"

"I'm not sure—" Hype began.

"Did you have to climb over the wall to get out? Or was there like a big escape through the gates, like with soldiers and spies and stuff?"

"No," said Hype. "No. That wasn't us. We—"

"We're on vacation," interrupted Dawk.

"In Dayton?" the kid said. "Why would anyone come here for vacation?"

"Well, we have to go now," Hype said.

"Wait a minute, what about the spork?" the guy said. "I was going to let you have it when you were from East Germany, you know, since I don't want to start any world wars or anything like that, but if you're not—"

"Okay, look, I'm pretty hungry, so why don't you go get us two coleslaws for the sporks, and we'll pay you and just go back to where we came from," Dawk suggested.

"You want sodas?"

"No," Dawk said. "Just sporks—I mean, just coleslaws."

"Be right back," the kid said, snapping his fingers and almost dancing back behind the counter.

Tell Benton now! *(Hype)*

Everything around them started to wrinkle, as if the atmosphere was thick as water. That was Benton, beginning the process of pulling them out of 1982.

The kid turned around. "Hey, you forgot to pay!"

But Dawk and Hype were gone.

CHAPTER 25

All the time-travel pit stops were making Hype's head spin. She left Dawk in the twenty-fifth century and was back to feudal Japan and the Neanderthal, who was still cowering in the back room. Hype wasn't sure how much time had passed in Japan since she'd left, but it couldn't have been more than a minute.

You do remember the plan, don't you? (Fizzbin)

Of course I do. (Hype)

Hype knew the plan. She just didn't how she'd explain it to Komatsuhime.

The Neanderthal was frightened out of his wits. "Just wait a second," Hype said, even though she knew he wouldn't understand her. She didn't want him to run off while she left the shop to speak to Komatsuhime.

Hype ran out of the rice cake shop to find the monk gone. Komatsuhime was patiently waiting for Hype with Shinobu at her side.

"I think I can solve all this," Hype told her, "but you need to trust me. I might ask you to do some crazy things, you might see me do some incredibly silly things, but I can promise you that everything will get back to normal soon. I think."

"Hypatia, you have nerves of steel," Komatsuhime said, "and a heart and brains to match. I will trust whatever you tell me."

Shinobu looked over at Komatsuhime with a raised eyebrow of concern.

"I'll be right back," Hype said, and she dashed back into the shop.

When Hype came back out, she was walking sideways, holding out the spork to the Neanderthal, who slowly followed her out of the shop. Shinobu gasped, but Komatsuhime was calm as she watched the Neanderthal.

"If anyone comes for him, I need you to protect him," Hype said. "I'm bringing him back to the castle. Please make sure that no one touches him on the way. I don't want him scared off."

"Of course," said Komatsuhime, and motioned to Shinobu to take up position behind the Neanderthal.

The Neanderthal was calm and a little playful as they headed toward the castle. Hype guessed that he was probably relieved.

As they walked, Hype kept the spork just out of his reach. She spoke to him kindly. "Don't you worry, Neanderthal man, you'll get your spork, yes, you will!"

She led the Neanderthal as far as the drawbridge. But then Nazo came barreling up from the town, with Chiyoye right behind him. Komatsuhime and Shinobu readied their naginatas for the worst.

"I have caught you with the tengu!" Nazo yelled. "And he doesn't even take the form of a boy this time, so I can see the big nose flopping around.

Hand him over, or I will call my brothers and sisters here to help me grab him!"

"This is not a tengu, monk," Komatsuhime said calmly. "It is some other creature. A creature I am dealing with and that you should leave alone."

Hype did her best to ignore them and keep leading the Neanderthal toward the castle. The man had a smile on his face, and he didn't seem to notice the argument behind him, he was so focused on Hype and the spork.

"Of course that is a tengu!" Nazo said. "That creature has followed me around on the mountain and in town and in your castle. It swoops down on me and causes me terror and woe!"

"How does he swoop without wings?" Komatsuhime asked.

"The wings are invisible when it walks. They only appear when it flies," Nazo said. "You don't need wings to swoop, anyhow. Don't test me about tengu! I tell you about tengu, you don't tell me!"

"He really does know an awful lot about tengu," Chiyoye said.

"Maybe they would like to come watch the

ceremony to expel the creature," Komatsuhime called to Hype. "Maybe that would put their minds at ease."

"You can't have a ceremony without me," Nazo said. "I'm the one who has the tengu-expelling ceremonies, not you, onna-bugeisha."

"He really is quite good at tengu expelling," Chiyoye said.

"Well, then, maybe he can help us out," Komatsuhime said. "Do you think he might be a big help to us, Hypatia?"

"We're crazy to think we could have done it without him!" Hype answered.

You've asked him to do what? (Fizzbin)

It was Komatsuhime's idea. I wasn't going to argue with her. (Hype)

I hope she knows what she's doing. (Fizzbin)

CHAPTER 26

It turned out that Dawk went back to Japan off-Link and with Backup Fizzbin secure in his neural bypass. Dawk wasn't thrilled. But Benton said that one family member needed to be capable of entering the vReality just to try to keep the Neanderthal calm while the rest of the plan played out.

Mom and Dad tried to console him. He might not be on-Link, but he'd had some unique adventures that day, so it wasn't all bad.

"I'd bet your vReality experience in 1692

Massachusetts was in a town called Salem," Dad said. "Virtual time travel. That's amazing!"

"Pretty soon Fizzbin will be traveling to data banks in other eras," Mom said. "I wonder if we'll even have a job anymore."

"We barely have a job now," Dad said, laughing.

Mom stopped and put her hand on Dawk's shoulder to pause him.

"I think you should know that Hype tells us that that horrible weirdo monk is following them and likely to show up with the Neanderthal," she said.

"I've got an idea of how to deal with him," Dawk said. "I'll need your help, though."

"What kind of help?" Dad said, raising an eyebrow.

"When Nazo shows up with Hype," Dawk said, "could you try to get him into the Forbidden Area? I might know how to scare him away from the castle."

"He sounds like an annoying little man," Mom said. "It will be our pleasure."

They walked together through the castle

together until they came to the kitchen, where they found Junko. "I was hoping you'd be back!" she said.

"This is Junko," he told his parents. "Junko, these are my parents."

"So you're the one who helped Dawk out when he couldn't quite roll out of the Forbidden Area," Mom said. "Thank you. I don't know what he would have done without you!"

"Mom, I could've rolled out of the Forbidden Area by myself," Dawk said.

"Maybe," Mom said. "But I'm glad Junko was there."

"We had better keep moving," Dawk said, walking on.

Junko came hurrying up behind him. "You are in quite a hurry," she said.

"I've got to meet my sister at the Forbidden Area," Dawk said. "She needs some help."

"I will be happy to help, if she needs it," Junko said. "Things have been much more interesting since your family came to the castle."

"I might have a job for you," Dawk said. "If you

want a job, that is. If you can take time away from the kitchen."

"Kitchen work is nice enough," Junko said, "but this is exciting. What is my job?"

Once they arrived in the Forbidden Area, Dawk and Junko walked into the room and sat quietly on the floor.

Fizzbin's backup appeared, this time taking on a custom avatar of a Neanderthal woman. They hoped the sight of something familiar might help the Neanderthal stay calm after he was lured into the Forbidden Area.

Their job—or, really, Fizzbin's—was to keep the Neanderthal calm so that Dawk's family could easily surround him, give Benton a fix on his location, and get him out of there.

"I still don't really understand what is going on," Junko said.

"Think of it like we're all having the same dream together," Dawk told her.

"I will try," Junko said. "But who is the strange woman in the animal skins? Why is she is having this dream also?"

"That's Backup Fizzbin. He's, um . . ." Dawk didn't quite know how to explain it.

"I'm here to make sure the dream turns out all right," Backup Fizzbin said.

CHAPTER

27

A strange parade shuffled through the halls of the castle, causing guards and servants alike to stand aside in confusion. Hype, the Neanderthal, Komatsuhime, Shinobu, Nazo, and Chiyoye continued through the halls, past the kitchen, and finally to the Forbidden Area.

"There they are!" Mom said. "Dawk is waiting in there already."

"That Neanderthal sure loves that spork!" said Dad, watching the man follow Hype.

Hype started backing into the Forbidden Area,

where Dawk and Junko were both sitting on the floor, staring blankly ahead.

"Are they okay?" Hype asked.

"They're just waiting for your hairy friend," Dad said.

Hype stopped in front of the door, and the Neanderthal lunged toward her. He grabbed the spork and dashed through the doorway.

But as soon as he entered the Forbidden Area, he stumbled down to the floor. The stream had connected to his primitive brain, and it was making him dizzy.

I guess we let Fizzbin's backup calm him down and then we triangulate. (Hype)

Hype started walking into the room. Mom and Dad were about to join her, but Nazo pushed them out of the way and barreled in.

"I demand to finish with the tengu by myself!" he yelled. But then he tripped over his own feet and fell on top of the Neanderthal.

Chiyoye began to take off after Nazo, but Komatsuhime quickly grabbed the woman's shoulder and held her back.

"We should watch from the doorway," Komatsuhime told her.

CHAPTER

28

Dawk watched as the Neanderthal and Nazo entered the Forbidden Area in vReality.

"There are two now?" said Nazo. "But there was only one when I looked in the room. The tengu must be scared! It had to call another one to help face me!"

"Nazo, there is a more powerful yokai hunter than you in the house," Dawk said.

"What do you know? You're just a yokai in disguise, that's all you are!" Nazo yelled. "You think I'm some stupid guy? I've got this all figured out!"

Nazo looked around the room, confused. "Where have the others gone?" he yelled. "Where's Chiyoye? Cowards! It's up to me to perform the ceremony to battle the tengu."

"Nazo, I'd like to introduce Junko," Dawk said. He motioned to the girl.

"Little girls can't vanquish a tengu." Nazo chuckled. "Now you're going for laughs."

I think it's time to unlock this vReality. A demon will enter, and your plan will begin. (Backup Fizzbin)

With only that warning, Backup Fizzbin took the lock off, and a vReality tengu burst out of nowhere, moving in for the whole crowd.

Dawk shielded Junko from the creature, but she stood up and looked like she was ready to face it on her own.

"So if I face this creature, it cannot hurt me?" Junko asked quietly.

"It's just like I said," Dawk told her. "It counts on you thinking it is there and real and terrifying. It's not really there. It just seems like it is."

Junko pointed to Nazo, who was running around the room, being chased by the vReality tengu.

"Then that monk is not doing a very good job of facing it," Junko said.

"You need to show him how to do it," said Dawk. "I have a plan."

Junko hurried over to where the tengu had Nazo cornered. The monk stood ready, but did not make any moves. It was like he was frozen in place.

Dawk thought his plan just might work. Junko might be able to help stop Nazo from causing any more problems by convincing him that he wasn't the most powerful yokai hunter around. Seeing the Neanderthal being transported away wouldn't convince Nazo of anything. He would still be a pain to Komatsuhime. This, though? This could work.

Junko ran up to the creature, which turned toward her. She did exactly as Dawk had instructed and placed her hand on the tengu's forehead. Then Backup Fizzbin locked the vReality again, and the tengu vanished into thin air.

Confused and slightly angry, Nazo looked at Junko.

"You think you are better than me, little girl?" Nazo sneered. "I have trained for this since childhood. Beginner's luck! What about those two tengu?"

Junko ran over to the Neanderthal and Backup Fizzbin next, reaching her hands out.

"We shall join hands," Junko said.

Backup Fizzbin placed his hand in Junko's, and the Neanderthal, watching carefully, did the same.

"You must go home now!" Junko commanded.

Suddenly, the Neanderthal was no longer in the room.

Dawk knew that meant out in reality, Hype, Mom, and Dad had managed to help Benton grab the Neanderthal into the future.

"Now I will deal with the real other tengu in the room," Junko said. She turned to Nazo, who looked at her in terror.

"You," Junko said to him. "We know your secret, tengu."

Dawk was just marveling at how great Junko was at scaring Nazo when he noticed that Backup Fizzbin was no longer there.

Backup Fizzbin, where are you? (Dawk)

I am following my programming. Part of me is

converting into a virus for the system connected to this stream. (Backup Fizzbin)

What does that mean? (Dawk)

Following my conversion into a virus, I will upload myself back on this system. All that will be left of me in your NeuroCache is the data I have acquired. In the meantime, this vReality stream will be shutting down momentarily. (Backup Fizzbin)

What happens then? (Dawk)

No time for that. One last thing. 3132. Remember that number. You have been there. (Backup Fizzbin)

Dawk found himself in the Forbidden Area. His mom and dad were there. So were Hype, Junko, and Nazo.

"She is dangerous!" Nazo yelled as he got to his feet. "She thinks I am a tengu!"

He scuttled to the doorway and grabbed Chiyoye's arm. "She is more powerful than you are," he said. "We must go."

Dawk elbowed Junko, who looked stunned. "Stop, tengu!" she called out.

"I can arrange an escort out for you," Komatsuhime said.

Shinobu stepped forward. "I know a shortcut back to the mountain," he told the monk.

CHAPTER 29

The word soon spread that the vandal had been caught, and the sight of Nazo making an escape to his mountain led to suspicious whispers around the castle town. By the end of the day, everyone in town believed that Nazo had been the culprit all along and that he had tried to fake a tengu attack so that he could trick his way into becoming a famed yokai hunter.

The monks who had followed him down to help him capture the tengu believed this story, too, but with a twist. It turned out that it was known in drama and folklore that tengu sometimes disguised themselves as monks. Nazo, the mountain monks decided, was obviously another case of that. His fanatical devotion to "The Long-Nosed Goblin of Kurama," it was believed, was a clue. His brother monks had no trouble putting all the pieces together, whether they were true or not.

Dawk figured Nazo was probably back up in the mountain battling giant squirrels.

The Faraday family would be headed back to the Alvarium soon, but it seemed that Japan would still have time travelers. The discovery of the strange temporal feed in the Forbidden Area had led Benton to theorize that there could be more feeds scattered around the country. What would be the point of just having one isolated set-up in an out-of-the-way castle?

And so a team of twenty-fifth-century investigators was combing through Japan, hoping to detect the feeds, destroy them, and gather more information about them.

With just days left, Dawk decided to spend his time with Junko. She wasn't anywhere near as stunned by their experiences as Dawk had worried she would be. In fact, she was energized, and most days, when Dawk met her after her kitchen shift ended, she wanted to head out to town and go yokai hunting.

"You're not exactly a real yokai hunter," Dawk said. "You just faked it to help get rid of Nazo."

"I know that," Junko said, smiling, "but that doesn't mean I don't want to learn."

CHAPTER

30

We think that in the confusion, the Neanderthal was transported back to his own time with the spork in his hand. We haven't been able to locate it, so that is the most likely explanation. (Fizzbin)

This didn't make Hype very happy. She had gone through so much to recover the spork, only to lose it again.

But doesn't that defeat the purpose of everything we've been through, trying to prevent an anomaly from happening? (Hype)

Benton informs me that there are more pressing

matters currently than the spork. He wants to assure you that there is no record, even in our own observations of prehistory, of early man developing any sort of plastics, or even copying the spork into a stone or wooden utensil with a similar form. (Fizzbin)

There were other things happening that needed Hype's attention more than the lost spork. When Lord Sanada returned and found that his wife had solved the crime spree, he was very happy. He arranged another tea ceremony when it came time for the Faradays to give their farewell. Before that, though, Hype had to talk to Komatsuhime about a few things in private. It was an excuse to take her naginata in hand one more time.

Komatsuhime didn't ask any questions about what had happened. Hype worried that what her friend had encountered would cause a disruption in history, but Komatsuhime accepted the unexplainable very calmly. The older woman was also happy that the experience had solved the problem of vandalism in the town and gotten Nazo out of her hair.

"The last Shinobu saw of him, he was making

a mad dash toward the mountains," Komatsuhime said. "That madwoman couldn't even catch up with him."

Hype's one regret about returning home was that she couldn't continue her training with Komatsuhime. Even with all the proper certification, Hype couldn't imagine the Chancellor allowing anyone from the twenty-fifth century to come back to train as a warrior.

In the meantime, Hype had another idea. "Dawk told me that Junko was very brave while facing the tengu and Nazo. She's the reason we were able to get rid of Nazo. If you'll take my word for it, that is. I know you didn't actually see any of the stuff that should have been happening in front of your own eyes, but trust me, it does make sense."

"I know it does, Hypatia," Komatsuhime said. "Mystery is just an aspect of life, part of essence. I certainly do not yet understand, and may never. But I do wonder: what interest is the bravery of a Japanese kitchen girl to you?"

"I'd like her to take my place after my family leaves," Hype said. "In training, I mean."

Are you sure this is a very good idea? (Fizzbin)

If Benton's not worried about a spork in the wrong era, I'm certainly not worried about an anonymous girl in feudal Japan getting onna-bugeisha training. (Hype)

Komatsuhime was momentarily silent, thoughtful. "That is, of course, not for you to decide," she finally said.

"If you'll excuse me being so direct, it seems to me that you were bored around here before we showed up, and you're going to go back to being bored after we leave," said Hype. "Besides, it would be a good deed that would reflect well on you! Her entire life is going to be spent in that kitchen, but you have it in your power to give her a little something extra. Why are guys the only ones who get to have fun around here?"

"Well, society demands that—"

"Komatsuhime, I'm not suggesting that you change all of society," Hype said. "I'm just asking that you do a little thing. The girl has a lot more to offer you than clean pots and pans, don't you think?"

"Society also demands that young women do not speak to their teachers like that." Komatsuhime frowned. "I can only hope that Junko has more a sense of respect than you do, Hypatia, otherwise I don't know how I'm going to be able to teach her anything. But I will try."

Hype reached over and hugged the older woman and, for the first time ever, wished she wasn't a time traveler so she could stay right where she was.

CHAPTER

31

The Faradays had barely been back in the twenty-fifth century for an hour—just enough time to get Dawk to the Neuro Systematics Trauma Center and have his neural bypass reinstated—when Benton insisted they come down to his lab.

Benton was almost frowning. His brow was definitely furrowed. And his hands were behind his back. The Faradays weren't used to him looking so serious.

Are we in trouble? (Hype)

I don't like the look of this one bit. (Dawk)

If we screwed up something, what more could they do to punish Mom and Dad? (Hype)

They could make them research the history of underwear. (Dawk)

"I felt it necessary to call you all here," Benton told them. He pressed a button on the tabletop device next to him, and two three-dimensional brains were projected into the room.

"You deserve some explanations after what happened in Japan, especially now that we're seeing how it fits in with the wider picture as we've come to understand it," he said. "These are scans the OpBot took of Komatsuhime and Sanada. Do you notice anything unusual about them?"

"Well, there's a little mark in the frontal lobe," Mom said, pointing.

"Sharp eyes, Zheng," Benton said. "Do you know what that is?"

"It looks to me like a neural bypass," Dad said.

"That's exactly what it is," Benton said, "and when we saw it, it concerned us all. A person from 1595 shouldn't have a neural bypass. They wouldn't be invented for centuries. The Chancellor ordered wider scans of others in Japan of equal position in society as Komatsuhime and her husband, and this is what we found."

The Imager started flashing different brain scans every few seconds. Each brain had a neural bypass in it.

"Others had them, too," Benton said "Strange, though. None of them were set up to receive, just transmit. I was curious about that, so I had all the OpBots we sent back sweep the areas, and I found that each neural bypass was near a temporal stream like the one you found. You see what's going on?"

"A neural bypass set to transmit would be enough to block those temporal streams from the people who had the neural bypasses, right?" asked Dawk.

He does learn something! (Fizzbin)

"Yes. Very good, Dawk," said Benton. "The higher-ups in society could not register the vRealities being streamed, while everyone else could. This certainly must have caused some unrest between the classes." He held up a neural bypass between his finger and thumb. "This is the one we retrieved from Komatsuhime's brain," he said. "The easiest way to collect these is to travel back to a point after the subject has been dead and laid to rest, and then grab it. Morbid, I know, but we do what we have to do to keep time flowing correctly."

I wouldn't want that job. (Dawk)

If Mom and Dad get demoted again, that's what they're going to end up doing, isn't it? (Hype)

I think underwear would be worse. (Dawk)

"I do have one question," Benton said. "Dawk, those vRealities you experienced with Fizzbin's backup. I believe you are aware of the times and places of those."

"Yeah," Dawk said. "Fizzbin—uh, Backup Fizzbin told me when we were in there."

I never would have done that. It's not meant to be common knowledge. (Fizzbin)

But you did do it! You but not you! (Dawk)

"Two of them were pretty unimportant," Benton said. "Just some isolated perceived encounters with monsters and aliens that never really caught on as acceptable science, and we'll be watching to make sure they don't. However, the other one . . ."

"Were we in 3132?" Dawk asked quickly, remembering the strange thing Backup Fizzbin had told him. "Was that it?"

"I'm sorry, Dawk, I don't know what you mean," Benton said. "I'm talking about the one with the snow on the ground."

"The old-fashioned one? With all the girls screeching and the weird little guys?"

"Yes, that one," Benton said. "It was in a place called Salem, Massachusetts. Are you familiar with anything that happened in a place with that name?"

"I saw a mod about it when I was younger," Hype said. "The town accused a lot of people of being witches."

"Exactly," Benton said. "The Salem Witch Trials. As Dawk's experience shows us, streams have been set up in Salem at that time. But for what purpose?"

"To make the situation worse?" asked Mom.

"No," Benton said. "To make the situation *happen*. The vReality stream created false experiences in people, and that set in motion the events of the Salem Witch Trials. This means that they—whoever they are—succeeded at something. Something major."

"What do you mean?" asked Dad.

"We ran it against our historical backups that we keep in the DataVerse and found something very, very disturbing. In earlier versions of our time stream, the Salem Witch Trials never happened. It was a peaceful time for the town of Salem. What you witnessed with the monsters and the girls was a successful attempt to tinker with history and make the tragedy an accepted part of history," Benton said.

"Can't we just change it back?" asked Hype.

It's not that simple. Extensive analysis needs to be done, paradox probability studies, and even then we may not have enough answers. Changing the events in Salem has affected other things throughout history, and we have no idea what. It all has to be handled in a temporally correct way. (Fizzbin)

"Exactly," said Benton. "This shows how dangerous these people are. We've found one instance where they've altered our reality. How many other plots have they hatched? How will we ever uncover them all? Have we already missed others?"

Is what's about to happen here what I think is about to happen here? (Dawk)

If Mom and Dad get this assignment, they are going to be the happiest parents in the world. No more shoes! No more grumpiness! (Hype)

"But nothing for you to worry about!" Benton smiled. He reached into a drawer and pulled out a weathered brown clump. It looked a little like a foot with a thick strip on the bottom. "See this? This shoe has one of the earliest rubber soles. You're all going to visit Lowell, Massachusetts, in 1898 to find out how this little wonder was created! Such an exciting time to witness in the history of footwear!"

It could be worse. (Hype)

Right. Underwear. (Dawk)

CHAPTER 32

The good thing about Lowell was that nobody had to wear the little Japanese sandals anymore. About a week into the mission, though, there still wasn't much for Dawk and Hype to do except for wandering and waiting and trying to make sense of what Benton had told them and what Dawk had seen in his journey through the future vReality streams.

One day, they were talking about all that same information, all over again, as they often did, when a black carriage pulled up beside them. A small window slid open and a very old man with great gray muttonchops and wild hair stuck his face out.

"Dawk. And Hype! My eyes do not deceive me!" he called out to them.

Is that someone we know? (Dawk)

He doesn't look familiar. We've never been here before, anyhow. (Hype)

"You told the truth," the man said. "You are here. I came to see for myself."

Both Dawk and Hype stood up. "What are you talking about?" asked Dawk.

"You said Pawtucket Street, next to Pawtucket Falls in Lowell, Massachusetts," said the man. "You gave me this date. Of course, I had no choice but to be here, right now at this particular moment. It is in your past. You remembered it happening, therefore it must have happened. At least, that is what you believe."

Dawk and Hype looked at each other. "We don't understand," Hype said.

"No, you don't," the man said, "because even though you travel back and forth in time, you don't understand what a mess time is." He smiled.

"You view it as one way or another way, but it's all ways, isn't it? It's always expanding and contracting and shifting, and you don't see that in the small picture. My family has learned that much over the centuries."

"Would you like to explain yourself?" asked Dawk.

"No," the man said. "I only came to confirm what I already suspected. You will know more soon enough. When you are meant to know more."

"Who are you?" asked Hype.

"My name is Marek Richthausen, but I am known in more lofty circles as Baron Chaos," he said. "We met fifty years ago, and we meet again today. You knew my great-great-great grandfather. You met him in Prague many centuries ago. You are such family legends. I cannot believe that I have now met you twice."

"You're Jan Richthausen's great-great-great grandson?" asked Dawk. "Someone actually married that weirdo?"

"And you pass down our story from generation to generation like some folktale?" Hype asked.

"That is weird. Why are you here? We really need to talk."

"No, no, no, now I must bid you adieu," the old man said. "I must return to my laboratories and factor in this information with all my calculations and the centuries of my family's research. I only came here to confirm what you told me."

"You can't go yet!" Hype said.

"But I must," Richthausen said. "Ready, driver!" He nodded to Dawk and Hype, and then he shut the window. The carriage rattled off.

So what was that about? (Dawk)

I suppose you'll find out fifty years ago, if what he says is correct. (Fizzbin)

Dawk and Hype both sat back down. The carriage was far down the road now, but if the old man was telling the truth, it carried in it a promise that their adventures were probably far from over. They listened to the roar of Pawtucket Falls and waited patiently for what would happen next.

ABOUT THE AUTHOR

John Seven grew up in the 1970s, when science fiction movies and TV shows were cheap and fun. His favorites shows were *The Starlost, Land of the Lost,* and *Return to the Planet of the Apes,* and he loved time travel most of all. John collaborated with his wife, illustrator Jana Christy, on the comic book *Very Vicky* and a number of children's books, including *A Year With Friends, A Rule Is To Break: A Child's Guide To Anarchy, Happy Punks 1-2-3,* and the multi-award-winning *The Ocean Story.* John was born in Savannah, Georgia, and currently lives in North Adams, Massachusetts, with his wife and their twin sons, Harry and Hugo, where they all watch a lot of *Doctor Who* and *Lost* together.